What Would Emma Do?

What Would Emma Do?

Eileen Cook

Simon Pulse
New York London Toronto Sydney

SIMON PULSE
An imprint of Simon & Schuster Children's Publishing Division
1230 Avenue of the Americas, New York, NY 10020

Designed by Mike Rosamilia
The text of this book was set in Cantoria MT.
Manufactured in the United States of America
First Simon Pulse edition January 2009
10 9 8 7 6 5 4 3 2 1
Library of Congress Control Number 2008930328
ISBN-13: 978-1-4169-7432-1
ISBN-10: 1-4169-7432-6

What Would Emma Do?

1

God, I've been thinking about our relationship. The way I see it, most people look at you as either (a) a Santa Claus figure they pray to only when they want something, their wishes granted depending on if they are on the naughty or nice list, or (b) a bearded vengeance seeker who gets his immortal jollies from smiting those who annoy him. It occurs to me I've been talking to you my whole life and I don't really know who you are. In fairness, I've always relied on formal prayers, which really haven't given you a chance to get to know me, either. I'm thinking we need a bit more honesty in our relationship—you strike me as the kind to support honesty—so from here on I'm just going to tell you what's on my mind.

We spend a lot of time at Trinity Evangelical Secondary discussing "What would Jesus do?" You have to wonder how the Son of God finds himself in so many ethically questionable situations. I'm guessing he hangs out with a bad crowd.

We've covered how Jesus feels about:

- low-rise jeans (negative)
- underage drinking (although this is the same man who brought us wine transformed from water, we've decided he would just say no)
- gossip (to be avoided—which goes to show he would never make it in Wheaton, where gossip has been perfected to near Olympic levels)

All in all, the Son of God is coming across as a very no-fun kind of guy. I prefer to see him as not so uptight. This puts me in the minority here, where the motto for our church could be "Trinity Evangelical: Sitting in judgment on others since 1849."

At the moment we were supposed to be discussing in great detail, as if this is an issue the president of the United States might need to consult us on, what Jesus would do if he accidentally came across the answers to the math test before the exam. Everyone stared off into space, pondering how our savior might handle this tricky situation.

I left the issue of exam ethics to my capable classmates and went back to trying to get my best friend Joann's attention. I risked a look over my shoulder at her. Mr. Reilly, our religion teacher, has been known to hurl erasers at the heads of students he feels aren't paying attention, so being subtle was key. Joann was either ignoring me or in a catatonic state. I gave a fake cough to draw her attention. Nothing. I coughed again, this time drawing it out as if I might be in the final stages of TB, but not even a glance.

Darci Evers raised one perfectly manicured hand in the air. Darci looks like she jumped out of a spread in *Seventeen* and the teachers always talk about how she makes a great role model, but don't be fooled. She's the kind of person who laughs if you trip in the cafeteria. If your mom forces you to wear the sweater your nearly blind grandmother knit for you, she gives a brittle, thin smile and says, "Nice sweater." Then her posse of friends giggle. In elementary school she dotted the *i* in her name with bubbles and hearts.

"If Jesus saw the test before the exam, he would tell the teacher and ask for a new test, one where he didn't know the answers," Darci said. She paused, her head cocked to the side as if she was getting direct communication from heaven. "Our Lord doesn't like cheaters."

I fought the urge to roll my eyes. The rest of the class all nodded, seemingly relieved to have this conundrum solved and Christ no longer at risk for blowing the hell out of the bell curve. Mr. Reilly smiled. He adores Darci Evers.

"Excellent answer."

I raised my hand. Mr. Reilly's smile withered.

"God is all-knowing, right?" I asked.

"Yes, Emma. He knows everything, what you've done and even what you will do." Mr. Reilly took this moment to look out over the classroom in case anyone had evil or impure thoughts in their hearts.

I looked to see if Joann was following my line of intellectual debate. Joann has never been a huge Darci fan, and I figured it wouldn't hurt to remind her that we had this in common.

"So if God knows everything, won't he know what questions the teacher is going have on the new test too?"

Mr. Reilly's head started to turn red, and I could see the vein in his forehead bulge. For a guy so close to Jesus, he has a lot of repressed rage issues.

"Are you trying to be smart?" Mr. Reilly said.

I hate questions like this. There is no right answer. If

you say you are trying to be smart, you get in trouble for being a wiseass, and if you say you're not, you're admitting to being stupid. It's what they call a lose-lose situation. What would Jesus do if faced with this question? I'm guessing he would go for honesty, but Jesus didn't have to worry about getting lower than a C in class and losing his track eligibility as a result.

"No, sir," I answered.

Mr. Reilly gave a snort and turned back to the board. Darci shot me a look of annoyance and raised her hand again. Joann still wasn't paying any attention to me.

"Mr. Reilly, do you mind if I make an announcement? It's related to student council business," Darci said.

Darci never misses an opportunity to make an announcement. She finds excuses in nearly every class to take center stage. I suspect that if it were up to her as senior class president, she would get to wear a small crown or sash to denote her overall superiority. I'm shocked she doesn't demand that the rest of us scatter palm fronds on the floor in front of her as she walks through the halls.

"As everyone knows, the big spring dance is coming up in just a few weeks, and we still need volunteers to help with the decorations. This year we've selected the theme 'Undersea Adventure.' Please show your school spirit by helping to make this a great event. Even if you haven't been asked to the dance, you could still decorate. We'll be accepting nominations for king and queen for the next two weeks, and the three couples that get the most votes will be announced as the court. The queen and king will be announced at the dance."

"I nominate you," Kimberly said so quickly she must have bumped her nose on the way to kissing Darci's ass.

Darci placed a hand on her heart as if she were overcome by the honor.

"Why, Kimberly, thank you so much! I feel a bit funny about putting myself down on the list, but if you insist." She pulled out her pink gel pen to inscribe her name before she forgot it.

"Why do we even have a king and queen?" I asked.

"We've always had a king and queen of the spring dance. It's tradition," Darci shot back.

"Maybe it's time for a new tradition." As the challenge shot out of my mouth, I couldn't tell who was more surprised, Darci or me. It felt like the air was sucked out of the room for a second as people held their breath, waiting for Darci to whack me back down to size. At least I had Joann's attention now.

"You can't have a new tradition. Then it's not tradition,

it's the opposite; it's new," Darci said, giving me a look, as if shocked that someone of my low intelligence was even allowed in school.

I slunk down in my seat.

"What would Jesus do?" asked Todd.

The entire class turned around to face him. Todd Seaver is the guy in our class who never says anything. There have been rumors that he's an elective mute. Todd has the dubious honor of being from "away," a non-Wheaton native.

"What are you talking about?" Darci asked.

"Would Jesus approve of people setting themselves above others? Sounds like false gods."

"It's not like that at all. Besides, you're Jewish, how would you even know what Jesus would do?"

There was a gasp. It's an unwritten rule that we don't bring up Todd's Jewishness. In a town that is all born-again, his religion is like a deformity, one of those things everyone is painfully aware of and tries to act like they don't notice.

"He was one of the tribe when he started out, you know," Todd said. "I'm thinking he would see the whole king and queen thing as a bunch of false idols, golden calves." He gave Darci a lazy half smile and then looked over at me.

I slunk farther down in my seat, not meeting his eyes. If I went any lower I would slide completely out of the chair and onto the floor. Part of me was glad someone else was standing up to Darci. I just wished the person I was aligned with wasn't the class pariah.

"Interesting point," Mr. Reilly said, tapping his thin fingers on his Bible. He adored Darci, but stamping out fun was his favorite thing in the world.

"It's tradition," said Darci, her voice cracking.

"I think we need to discuss the dance at the next advisory board meeting," Mr. Reilly said as the bell rang.

Darci's mouth opened and shut silently like a fish flopping on a dock. A fish with pink-bubble-gum-scented lip gloss. Everyone got up and moved toward the door. I stood up and grabbed my bag.

Darci bumped into my back. "Way to go, Emma," she hissed, shoving past me.

"Yeah, way to go," Kimberly parroted, following two steps behind her.

Joann walked up next to me, and I gave her a smile.

"My mom already bought me a dress for the dance," she said, crossing her arms. "Why can't you leave some things alone?" She walked away without another word.

Recent events, combined with years of religious study, have clarified for me that at the ripe age of seventeen, I am pretty much already damned to hell. Let's recap:

The Seven Deadly Sins

- Gluttony: I have, on more than one occasion, eaten the entire gut-buster ice-cream sundae at the Dairy Hut that you get for free if you can finish it. What can I say? I run a lot; I get hungry.
- Greed: I have a passion for my running shoe collection that others might reserve for the members of a boy band. It's not just fashion; it's also about function.
- Sloth: Every time my mom sees the state of my room, she is compelled to say, "If you're waiting for the maid to come along, you've got a long wait ahead of you." Then she sighs deeply, like being my mother is her burden in life.
- Wrath: I detest Darci Evers, and if I had the opportunity it is quite likely I would replace her shampoo with Nair.
- Envy: I would give just about anything, including possibly my soul, to run like Sherone Simpson (ranked number one in the world for the hundred meters).

- Pride: I won the state championship last year for hurdles and plan to repeat this year. I've been accepted to Northwestern, and if I can nail down a track scholarship, I've even got a way to pay for it and a way out of town.
- Lust: I kissed my best friend's boyfriend over Christmas break.

Yep, it's pretty much the last one that's going to do me in.

2

God, I know you're busy, and to be honest, what with famine, pestilence, and war I feel a bit bad about bugging you in the past over silly things like getting breasts (although—hey, it's never too late), but the situation with Joann is really bugging me. Is there any way you could remind her that we're best friends? A small vision, perhaps? I really am sorry for what happened with Colin. Think of the benefits: If we were close again, I wouldn't need to come to you with the small things, I could sort them out with her. Consider it less like granting a prayer and more like a time-saving device for yourself.

There is no greater sin than kissing your best friend's boyfriend. It's such an obvious screwup it didn't even make the Ten Commandments. God figured he shouldn't even have to make a note of that one.

I've known Colin since I was two, which is long before he started dating Joann. Not that I'm trying to offer that up as an excuse, more of an explanation. After my parents divorced, my mom (for reasons that have never been clear to me) moved us from Chicago (a perfectly good city without a single silo, which is more than I can say for Wheaton) to live near her parents, my grandparents. Colin's family farm is right next to my grandparents. We grew up together with everyone making smoochy kissy noises around us with elaborate winks and nudges. His dad and my grandpa would always joke about how the fence between their two farms could come down with no trouble at all. Then there's the humiliating childhood photo that gets pulled out every so often, of the two of us around age five sharing a bath. It was expected that we would become a couple, which pretty much guaranteed it was the last thing that either of us would ever want. In a small town like Wheaton, it is an accepted fact that getting married is the high point of your life. Big church wedding with big hair and a big bouquet and then a bad buffet at the Veterans' Hall. Shoot me.

Even though I never planned to date Colin, I always liked him. I don't mean *like him* like him. Just regular like. He's a good guy. He doesn't mind renting chick flicks, and he introduced me to the Matrix movies (which despite having Keanu Reeves are pretty good). He's into football, but if I ask, he'll watch me run on the track, and he'll scream out my times as I fly by. Since I've known him forever, I can tell him stuff without feeling like I'm talking to a guy. He'll tell you the truth about how you look in stuff (like if your jeans make your ass a mile wide). Colin even asked me what I thought about him asking Joann out this past summer before he did it. I did the emotional reconnaissance for him, so he knew she would say yes. I was glad they hit it off. Honest.

It was my idea to drive into Fort Wayne and go to the mall at Christmas. Wheaton is so lame we don't have a mall. There is one clothing store in town, the Hitching Post. All their clothing smells like old people and has an elastic waist. Wheaton is not exactly fashion central. Colin was trying to figure out what to get Joann for Christmas. They had been dating since July, and this was their first major "couple" holiday, which put on the pressure for gift giving. The Hitching Post was not going to cut it. A trip to a real shopping destination was required, and who better to help him with the gift selection than his girlfriend's best friend?

The mall was insanely busy. They had decorated with huge garlands covered with ornaments the size of border collies strung between the stores, and there was a giant winter wonderland in the center. A single loop of Christmas songs kept repeating over and over. Every time you walked into a store, one of the clerks would yell, "Season's greetings!" in this frantic voice like they'd had one too many rounds of eggnog. Colin was starting to drag, and I could see he was ready to buy something and leave. I gestured to the Gap up ahead and started to lead Colin into the store.

"Let's go sit on Santa's lap instead," Colin said, pulling me down the slick white floor.

"Santa? Don't you think we're a bit old?"

"You're never too old for Santa."

Colin was practically racing down the hall. We stood in line for Santa with all the little kids. The kid in front of us had his finger jammed up his nose and watched us warily while doing his nasal drilling. I tried to ignore him.

"What are you leaning toward getting Joann?"

"I can't decide. What do you think of the sweater?"

"She'd like it."

Colin sighed.

"What? She would. She looks nice in green," I offered.

"There must be something that she'd really like. A sweater seems boring. I mean, I got my mom a sweater."

"Well, don't get Joann the same one. That's creepy."

"Thanks, Freud," Colin grumped, and then pushed me forward. Santa could see me now.

I sat down slowly on Santa's lap. The last thing I needed

to do was hurt the old guy. Up close he didn't look that old. Nor were his eyes very twinkly. However, he was built for the part: His belly had definite jellylike status. I think sitting on Santa's lap used to be better when I was a kid, or else I was too young to notice the ick factor back then.

"What do you want for Christmas?" Santa asked with what looked an awful lot like a leer to me.

"Santa?" Colin asked, his voice low and serious. Santa and I both turned to face Colin, who was standing next to the elf photographer. "Santa, why have you taken Christ out of Christmas?"

I burst out laughing just as the camera flashed. I thanked Santa for his time and chased after Colin, who was dancing near the printer, waiting for the photo. When it came out, it was worse than I expected. My mouth was wide-open, midlaugh, and my eyes were squeezed shut. Santa looked confused and annoyed. I gave Colin a shove. The elf assistant gave us a look, and I noticed that Santa was getting up to take a break. I'm guessing minimum wage was not cutting it to put up with people like Colin and me.

"Must you torture Santa?" I asked. Colin grabbed the photo and paid for it.

"Christmas is more than shiny paper and Rudolph. I

would hope as a student—no, an ambassador—of TES, you would know that. Have you forgotten the real reason for the season? Has Satan won you with nothing more than a shiny jingle bell and some cookies?" Colin asked in a solemn voice before his face cracked into a smile.

"Lemme see the picture again." I took it out of his hands. "I look like someone who wanders around with tinfoil on her head."

"No, you don't. You look good." He took the picture back.

"Good? My mouth is hanging open, and see that shiny bit there? I think that's drool. I drooled on Santa."

"You never like your pictures. It's nice."

"You're a freak. Tear it up."

"I'm not tearing it up, I paid for it."

"Just because you were dumb enough to pay for it doesn't mean I want a picture of me like that hanging around." I reached for the photo, and Colin held it above his head. He's annoyingly tall, so I was reduced to jumping up and down trying to snatch it from him.

We were laughing, and Colin kept yanking the picture just out of my grasp. I leaned in to try and take it. Suddenly our faces were inches apart, and then he kissed me.

Or I kissed him.

It's possible we met in the middle. The picture fell out

of his hand and drifted down to the floor like an autumn leaf. We just stood there, looking at each other.

I think if things had been different, we might have walked away and acted like it never happened. The whole thing was weird, some kind of space-time vortex, like on sci-fi shows when the screens gets all wavy and wiggly to indicate reality isn't what it used to be. I really think we would have just left, gone to get the sweater for Joann, and maybe stopped at the food court for a burger. However, that isn't what happened, because right behind us, with a front-row seat for the kiss, was Joann's mom.

3

God, one of the things I wonder about is why you seem to like some things better than others. For example, you make some people beautiful and some people look like a bad Mr. Potato Head practical joke. It would be one thing if the ugly people got to be smarter than the good-looking people, or luckier, but it doesn't always work that way. In fact, a lot of the time it seems pretty random. It's not just people—it's towns, too. Why is it places like Paris and New York have all the great nightlife spots, museums, and fancy bridges or buildings, and the only charm Wheaton has to offer is fireplugs painted like cartoon characters? Or if there must be places that have no redeeming features, why do I have to live in one of them? I know life isn't fair, but really, is it asking too much that you be?

How you know you live in a small town:

1. Someone writes a letter to you and puts only your name on the envelope and the mailman still knows *exactly* where to deliver it, even without the address.
2. The tallest buildings in town are the grain silo and the church steeple.
3. Everyone knows everyone else, also everyone else's parents, grandparents, and great-grandparents. Most likely everyone's great-great-grandparents sat next to each other on the Mayflower.
4. If in third grade you once laughed while taking a drink of milk and it sprayed out of your nose, everyone remembers this, and someone has a picture.
5. It is completely normal to play in the middle of the street as a kid, because traffic is a freakish event. As a small kid, you may take years to learn to look both ways when crossing the street, because you had no idea it was a needed skill.
6. Your town has no major retail outlets, no Gap, no Abercrombie, no Claire's, no McDonald's, no Dairy Queen, no nothing. If a Wal-Mart moves in a couple towns over, this event is greeted with

nearly as much excitement as the Rapture.

7. Going anywhere that has more than four traffic lights is called "going to the city."
8. If you wear something other than jeans, people around town will ask why you are getting "all dressed up."
9. The town has a cheesy catchphrase like "Welcome to Wheaton . . . the heart of Indiana." They're so proud of this they post it on a sign coming into town, like a warning to outsiders not to get off the highway.
10. Even if you travel an hour away from your small town and do something really foul, like accidentally kiss your best friend's boyfriend, someone who knows you will see.

Colin and I didn't talk much on the ride home. We sat in his truck, the vinyl seats freezing cold. His truck was a hand-me-down from his brother, and the radio got only the AM stations, so we listened to talk radio. I was hoping for better advice than "Go do the right thing!" That boat had already sailed.

I'm guessing that Joann's mom broke the sound barrier racing home. By the time Colin dropped me off,

Joann already wasn't speaking to me. Over the Christmas break Colin convinced her it was a weird once-in-a-lifetime freak accident—a case of lip hit-and-run. He and I never talk about it. Although to be fair, we never really talk about anything anymore; we more or less avoid each other. Colin and Joann stayed together, and officially Joann and I made up, but you can't be friends with someone since first grade and not know she's still a bit pissed at you. Can't say I blame her.

4

God, is it possible that you created certain people just to test me? Or is it possible the entire reason I exist is to annoy others? It seems to come easy to me sometimes, like it was destiny.

The cafeteria at TES is decorated with posters made by the Spirit Squad! (exclamation point required). TES doesn't have cheerleaders. The school's parent advisory board determined years ago that cheerleading is too sinful. Those short skirts, jumping around, dancing and thrusting to music—the devil's work for certain. Darci, who was clearly destined from birth to be the type of girl who would have school-color-coordinated ribbons tied in her hair and an overly perky personality, needed to find a way around the cheerleading ban. She came up with the idea of the Spirit Squad (!) whose job it is to promote school spirit and the Holy Spirit all in one go.

The Spirit Squad (!) makes motivational posters for the halls: "Jesus loves those who love others!" or "TES: The Best!" in annoyingly bright poster paint colors.

At the other end of the cafeteria from the "Go Crusaders!" banner is a giant floor-to-ceiling poster of Jesus. He's got his arms out like he wants to give you a hug—or maybe he's shrugging. I've always felt bad for him trapped in here where there's a distinct smell of old dishrags and sauerkraut. One of the cafeteria ladies is German and believes that any meal is improved with the addition of fermented cabbage. If I were the Son of God, I would not plan any Second Coming until the sauerkraut issue was dealt with. I bring my lunch.

Joann sat down with her tray and yanked up her knee-highs. As long as I've known Joann she's had this bizarre problem with elastic in her socks. She's the Bermuda Triangle of sock elastic. She can pull on a pair of new socks, and within ten minutes the socks will lie limp and saggy around her ankles. This wouldn't be a tragic affliction except for the fact that we go to a school that has a uniform that includes plaid skirts and knee-highs. Joann pushed the sauerkraut to the far side of her tray with her fork and gave the ham slice a tentative poke.

"Do you want part of my sandwich?" I asked, holding out my lunch as a peace offering.

"You sure?"

"Yeah, no problem." I tore my sandwich in half and gave her the larger piece. Joann took it and carefully parted the bread to check the contents before taking a bite. I've been known to like some odd combinations like mayo and dill pickle on rye. Of course, in Wheaton anything outside of bologna and mustard is considered odd.

"I didn't know you got a dress already," I said.

"Yeah. We went last weekend."

"That's cool."

I waited to see if she would describe it, but she didn't say a word. We sat in silence. I looked around. Colin was across the room at the jock table. He and a couple of other guys from the football team were laughing and pretending to hold each other up with a few sad-looking bananas filling in as guns. Suddenly I became aware that Joann was watching me. I knew she could tell I had been looking at Colin, and I felt as guilty as if I had been undressing him with my eyes instead of watching him act like a dork.

"Hey."

Both Joann and I looked up to see Todd Seaver

standing there. He had his hands jammed deep in his pants pockets. Todd is one of those kids who looks like he was created with a home Frankenstein kit. His legs are super-long, and he looks like he never knows what to do with his hands. His eyes are this amazing bright green, and then he has these thick eyebrows. His face has sharp lines, as if someone a bit dangerous drew him. He isn't ugly and he isn't hot, but he doesn't look like he belongs together. My mother would say he needs to grow into his looks.

"Nice call with the king and queen thing," Todd said. We stared at him. This was the most I'd heard from Todd ever in the entire time we'd gone to school together. I paused to see if he was going to say something deeply meaningful. You would think since he had been silent for so long he would have been saving up to say something profound, but it didn't look like it.

"Thanks," I said. We nodded at each other, apparently having run out of things to say. Our heads kept bopping up and down like we were listening to music.

"Cool, then." Todd wandered off.

"This is your ally against Darci?" Joann asked.

"Darci and I aren't at war."

"You should tell her that. Haven't you learned by now

that any questioning of the status quo is a declaration of war?" Joann pulled up her socks again. "Making fun of Darci is one thing, but getting in her way is another."

"I wasn't trying to get in her way, I swear. I asked one little question about the dance." I held my finger and thumb close together to show just how small a question.

"That dance is a sacred ritual as far as she's concerned."

"Once in a while someone has to stand up and point out if the status quo is full of it."

"Your funeral. Are you going to the Barn tonight?"

"Maybe. Depends who goes. How about you?"

"I can't, my parents are on the family night kick again." We rolled our eyes in tandem. Family night was the idea of Reverend Evers, who decided the decline of civilization was due to the fact that parents didn't play enough board games with their kids. Poverty, pestilence, rising greenhouse gases—all could be cured with a few rounds of Clue. Terrorism? Well then, it must have been Colonel Mustard in the library with a pipe bomb.

"Why do your parents want to do family night on a Friday? Can't it be on a Tuesday or something?"

"My dad bowls on Tuesdays." Joann shrugged. She isn't the kind to cause a lot of trouble at home. She doesn't even hang posters in her room, because her dad worries about holes in the wall or the tape ruining the paint. Even before the whole kissing Colin thing, I'm pretty sure her parents didn't like me. I have bad influence written all over me as far as they're concerned.

"You should come over," Joann offered suddenly.

"For family night?"

"It will be fun."

"Playing Candy Land will be fun? Your sister cheats."

"She's five."

"Uh-huh. Make excuses for her if you want. This is how people start down the road to ruin, excuses and excuses."

Joann gave me a shove. Her kid sister is, if possible, even better behaved than Joann. At five she already says please and thank you. I think I was still chewing on the furniture when I was her age.

"Well, if you don't want to come over, you could rent a movie and just chill. I mean, you probably want to take it easy. You've got a track meet tomorrow."

"Why the sudden concern over my social life?"

"I'm not concerned. You're the one who's all rabid about your track times this year and how that will determine the size of your scholarship."

Joann started to tidy up her tray, folding the paper napkins into smaller and smaller pieces.

"Do you not want me to go out for some reason?" I asked.

"No." Joann tossed her hair and looked out the window. She stood up and picked up her tray like she was ready to leave, and then sat back down. She was chewing on her lower lip. "Okay, yes. I don't want you to go to the Barn."

"Colin's going, huh?"

"Did he tell you that?"

"No, I'm just guessing that's why you don't want me to go."

"I don't like you guys hanging out."

"We used to hang out all the time and it never bothered you."

"That was before you kissed him."

That pretty much killed the conversation. She was right. I balled up the trash and stuck it in my lunch bag.

"Don't be mad," she said.

"I'm not mad, but you have to know I would never do anything like that again. Ever."

"I never thought you would do it in the first place."

"I said I was sorry." My voice came out tight. I was getting the idea that no matter how many times I said I was sorry, no matter how many ways I said I was sorry, it was never going to be better. I was always going to be the friend who kissed her boyfriend. God, I suck.

"If you want to go, go ahead," Joann said suddenly.

"I don't want to go."

"No, seriously, I'm being an idiot. You should go."

"I don't want to. Hanging out in an empty barn? Boring."

"It'll be fun. It's the first time anyone is going out there this year. You should go for both of us."

"No, you were right; I've got track tomorrow."

Joann opened her mouth to beg me to go again, and suddenly we both started to laugh. When I really get laughing, I snort, so the next thing you know I was snorting away, which just made Joann laugh more. The bell rang and we had to run to class, but she shot me a smile as we went into the room, and suddenly I had hope that it was going to work out. Then again, I've been wrong before.

5

God, I know that my mom used to be young. I've seen pictures of her at my age, so I know she wasn't born a forty-year-old mom. So what happened that caused her to completely forget what it was like? It's like she has teenage amnesia. Will it happen to me when I get old? Actually, come to think of it, there are plenty of things I wouldn't mind forgetting ever happened.

My mom and I used to get along great. We liked the same foods: Italian, anything with cheese, chocolate, and toast done really toasty and bordering on burnt. We hated the same things: overripe bananas, reality TV shows, control top pantyhose, and country music. We liked doing the same things: running, watching old movies, and reading fashion magazines. I even look a lot like my mom; we have the same brown hair (boring middle brown—not chestnut, not nearly blond, but Crayola crayon brown), green eyes (best feature hands down), and whippet-thin bodies. I know it's annoying when people say, "I can eat anything I want," but I can. It doesn't hurt that I run all the time, but my mom doesn't run that much and she's still thin. It may cut the envy to know I have no boobs whatsoever. Seriously, I am breast stunted. I have seen small male children with more of a bosom than I have. I have this theory that I was exposed to pesticides as a child. My mom used to let me run around on my grandparents' farm even after they had the crops dusted. Clearly they used some kind of breast-inhibiting chemical. You hear about stuff like this all the time on *Dateline*. I guess I should consider myself lucky that I don't have a third arm growing out of the middle of my forehead.

About a year ago, despite all we have in common, my mom and I started to get on each other's nerves. She says I developed an attitude. I'm fairly sure it's the same attitude I always had. If I had to guess, I'd say the problem is Wheaton. My mom loves this town. I hate it. My mom grew up in Wheaton and feels that moving away was *the biggest mistake of her life*. She thinks I have "rose-colored glasses" on when I talk about wanting to live in the city and that "the grass is not always greener on the other side of the fence." After all, "Small towns have big hearts." When my mom is upset, she talks in clichés. If you really want to tick her off, be sure to mention it. Because moving away didn't go well for my mom (and if you ask me, it wasn't moving away, it was making some tragically poor dating decisions), she's convinced it won't go well for me. Lately it feels like we're speaking different languages and anything can turn into a fight.

"I wanted to ask you something," my mom said, sitting down across from me on the sofa. She had on her serious mom face. Great. So much for my quiet, relaxing night before the track meet.

"Okay," I said, sitting up and waiting to hear what new thing she's discovered is wrong with my attitude.

"I found something in your room."

"What were you doing in my room?" My voice came out high and a bit screechy. It's not like I was hiding drugs or porn in there, but there was plenty of other stuff I would rather my mom didn't get her hands on.

"Can you explain this?" My mom pulled out a calendar from behind her back like she was starring in an episode of *Law & Order*. I had made it at the beginning of the school year. It showed each month between the first day and graduation. Each day I crossed off with a big black Sharpie marker.

"It's a calendar," I offered taking a deep breath. Here I had been worried she had found the stuff I had hidden under the bed. The calendar was nothing. Maybe she thought I was using the paper to roll cigarettes or something. She gave a sigh.

"I do not understand your hatred for this town."

"Whenever I try to explain it to you, you get mad."

"I get mad because you're building castles in the air and don't have your feet on the ground."

"Castles in the air?" I asked. Great, now she was starting to sound like the weird seventies ballads she loves. Soon she'd start talking about nights in white satin and horses named Wildfire.

"I know you've got your heart set on Northwestern. And I'm thrilled you got in—it's quite an accomplishment—but we don't have the money for out-of-state tuition. We're talking tens of thousands of dollars every year. Even if you get some assistance, I don't see how we could afford it. I don't want you to set your heart on something that isn't going to happen."

"That's why I'm going to get a full-ride scholarship. You might have noticed I've been doing this running thing?"

"Attitude."

I caught myself just before I rolled my eyes. I managed to

look down instead without saying anything. If she knew the whole story, she would freak out. The only place I'd applied was Northwestern. I have a bunch of other college applications, all filled out, stuffed under my mattress. If finding the calendar freaked her out, I could only imagine how she would feel if she found those. I know it's crazy to "put all my eggs in one basket," as my mom would say, but applying to other places felt like cheating on Northwestern. It's risky counting on them giving me a full ride for track, but it felt like I should take the risk, since I'm asking them to take a risk on me. Not to mention that I've been training like mad and plan to impress the hell out of them with my times. Somehow I knew my mom wouldn't see the logic in this plan.

"You know most of your friends will go to the Purdue extension campus in Fort Wayne," she hinted, as if that was a huge draw.

"If the rest of my friends jumped off a bridge, would you want me to?"

My mom's eyes narrowed. Okay, that last part might have had a bit of attitude, but honestly, aren't parents supposed to want you to reach for the stars? Isn't it like cheating for them to encourage you to settle?

"I am not going to have this discussion with you," she said.

"You were the one who sat down and said you wanted to talk with me. What's the big deal? I don't even know what you want from me anymore."

"What I want is for you to stop making this town into the enemy."

"I don't think it's the enemy, I think it's boring. I think nothing happens here. I want to live someplace where everyone doesn't know me. Where not everyone thinks they have a right to have an opinion on my life. I want to live someplace where there are restaurants that would never even consider having meat loaf on the menu. I want to live someplace where things happen."

"Oh, things happen in the city, all right. You just assume everything that happens will be good and exciting. There's something to be said for living someplace where people are concerned about you. Where you can count on someone looking out for you."

"Looking out for me or sticking their nose in my business?"

"Is this about what happened between you and Colin?"

"Mom!" I buried my head in my hands and wished I had never told her what happened. Somehow the kiss controversy had stayed a secret, but it wouldn't if my mom kept insisting on bringing it up.

“I know things can be complicated at your age. Sometimes we make mistakes.”

“Just because you made a bunch of mistakes doesn’t mean I will, and maybe I don’t need someone to watch out for me.”

As soon as the words shot out of my mouth, I wanted to pull them back in and swallow them down. My mom’s face went pale, and she sat back as if she didn’t want to be too close to me.

My mom and I never talk about my dad. I know the basics. He wasn’t what you would call a “stand-up guy.” He and my mom got married as soon as she found out she was pregnant, but settling down didn’t agree with him, and after a couple of years, they split up. Apparently, my terrible twos must have been pretty terrible. He was never the kind of guy to show up on weekends and try to spoil me by giving me too much fast food and sugar. He didn’t show up at all. When I was really little, he used to send presents at Christmas and on my birthdays, but that stopped around the time I outgrew Barbie’s dream castle. He dropped off the face of the earth, and neither my mom nor I could be bothered to find him. It’s hard to miss something you never had.

“Well, since you know it all, I’ll spare you my advice.”

She clicked on the TV and crossed her arms over her chest.

I jumped up and ran to my room, slamming my door behind me. It didn't make me feel any better, but it felt like the thing to do. Yep, that's right. Just some quality family time here at Chez Proctor.

6

God, according to our religion there is no such thing as reincarnation, and yet I have the sense that I must have done something in a previous life that really ticked you off . . . like killing missionaries or Bible burning. It's the only thing that makes sense for why you seem to have it out for me. If I promise to be better in my next life, will you lay off in this one?

The problem with running off to my room to make a statement is there's nothing to do once I get there. There's only so long I can lie dramatically across my bed. If my mother didn't force me to live in the Dark Ages, I would have a computer and my own phone line in here. Forget about cell phones. My mom believes it is "absurd" for anyone to need a phone they can carry around. She says no one needs that much immediate gratification. Our computer has to sit in the living room so that my mom can keep an eye on things and ensure I'm not trolling porn sites or chatting up creepy guys. My room is like something out of *Little House on the Prairie*. I suppose I should consider myself lucky that she lets me have electric light. I lay looking up at the ceiling where I'd pinned up a picture of Johnny Depp. There are worse things in life than waking up to Johnny. However, he wasn't much of a conversationalist. I rolled over and looked at my clock. Eight thirty p.m. No way in hell I was going back out there to sit on the sofa with my mom and act like a happy dysfunctional family.

I wandered around my room, kicking some laundry out of my way, and surveyed the options. I could spend my Friday night organizing my closet or work on some homework, thus cementing the fact that I have absolutely no life. I ran my finger along my bookshelf, but I've read everything on it at least once. I pulled the college applications out from under my mattress. I'd missed the application deadlines for everything except the extension campus in Fort Wayne. There was no turning back now. I tore the applications into tiny confetti-sized pieces and buried them deep in my trash can. I flopped onto the floor and did a few stretches and looked at the clock again—8:38.

I stood and pressed my ear against the door. I could hear the theme music for one of Mom's cooking shows drifting down the hall. Even though she almost never cooks, she has an obsession with watching other people cook. She watches the Food Network nonstop. I think she might have a thing for Jamie Oliver. The doorknob was cool in my hand, and I twisted it slowly, making sure the click was nearly silent. I slunk down the hall and grabbed the phone off the charger in the kitchen and slipped back into my room. I lay pressed against the door as if I had returned successfully from a spy mission.

I waited until my heart slowed down and then I called Joann. The phone rang only once and then their machine picked up.

"You've reached the Delaneys! Tom, Kathy, Scott, Joann, and Heidi. We can't take your call, but leave a message."

Each member of the Delaney family said their own name for the message in a perky *Sound of Music* Von Trapp family voice. Mr. Delaney is really into doing things as a family. Every year at Christmas they take a family picture with everyone wearing matching sweaters. If I were a sheep, I would protest this use of wool. Their family always has Sunday dinner together. Always. And never in front of the TV. They sit at the dining room table and hold hands while they say grace. Their family is frighteningly functional. It doesn't strike me as normal. I knew they were home, no doubt playing another round of Candyland, but they weren't going to pick up and interrupt their valuable family bonding time.

I clicked off the phone and sat on the floor next to the bed, pulling Mr. Muffles into my lap. Mr. Muffles is a stuffed dog that I've had since I was a kid. He used to be white with black ears and tail, but he hasn't aged well. He's a sort of gray color all over now. No Botox or eye lift for Mr. Muffles. One ear is flat and worn down. Apparently I used to suck on it as a kid. You couldn't pay me to put that ear in my mouth now, but when things are really stressing me out, I admit to rubbing it back and forth on my cheek. It is strangely soothing. Who am I to argue with what works? Maybe it's juvenile to keep Mr. Muffles now that I'm grown up, but what am I supposed to do, just throw him away? I don't think so. Despite recent events, that isn't how I treat friends. Problem is, my friend isn't answering the phone. It isn't that I don't have other friends; I hang out with a few of the other girls from track, but we're not the call-each-other-up-to-do-things kind of friends.

I tapped the phone on my knee as I thought over my options. Joann didn't want me to go to the Barn, but that was because she was still freaking out over the whole Colin thing, which was a total one-time-only accident. If she would answer the phone, I would go over there, but apparently she was engrossed in the great Candyland Olympics, which didn't leave me a whole lot of things to choose from. I tapped out Colin's cell number and waited for it to ring.

"Where are you?" I asked when he picked up.

"Em?" Colin sounded shocked to hear me. Fair enough, I hadn't called him without Joann around since the great Christmas kiss incident three months ago.

"Can you come get me?" My voice came out wavy as my throat tightened.

"On my way. Meet me at the corner." Colin clicked off.

That was one of my favorite things about Colin. He didn't waste time asking a bunch of stupid questions like, "Are you okay?" when it was crystal clear I wasn't. I yanked on a pair of jeans and pulled on my I ♥ NY sweatshirt. Not that I had ever been to New York, but with the wonders of the Internet you can order anything. I stuffed my bed with some of my laundry so it looked like I was curled up, sound asleep, and clicked off the lights.

I stood on my desk and slid open my window. One of the benefits of ground-floor living is the easy emergency access, and this was totally an emergency. I paused, waiting to see if I heard anything coming from the living room. Just Jamie Oliver blathering on about the wonders of olive oil. I swung one leg out and then the other. Once I was outside, I slid the window almost all the way closed and crouched to scurry down the driveway. I could see the lights in the living room and the outline of my mom sitting on the sofa. With any luck she would be too pissed to check on me.

The lights from Colin's truck swung around the corner. He coasted to a stop, and I ran up. I grabbed the handle and looked in at him through the window. His hair hung in his eyes. I had the sudden feeling that this was a mistake, and I paused. He looked at me, waiting. Well, this wouldn't be the first mistake I'd made.

I jumped into the truck cab.

7

God, here are the things I would do if you would let me develop real breasts. Real being defined as breasts having any size or dimension. We're not talking Pam Anderson here—I would happily settle for a nice B cup.

- *Feed the homeless on all major holidays*
- *Learn to sing and join the church choir*
- *Never show them off in a lewd manner*
- *Say a prayer of thanks on a nightly basis*

Please, God, do not let me continue to be the only girl in my class to be completely breast deprived. You are not supposed to give us any trials that we are not strong enough to endure, and trust me, I am not strong enough for this one.

I told Colin about the fight with my mom as we drove out to the Barn.

"It's like she won't be happy unless I'm unhappy," I said.

"She can't understand why you don't want to stay here," said Colin. He gestured outside the truck with a wave of his hand. "How could you leave all this behind?"

We were passing through downtown Wheaton. Downtown consists of all of one stoplight (which blinks after seven p.m.), the Hitching Post, the Veterans' Hall, Sheer Wonder hair salon, the bank, the Stop & Shop (which has the post office counter inside), and the Get Away (the fine dining experience in Wheaton—provided your definition of fine dining includes paper napkins and chicken-fried steak). After eight p.m. the town shuts down. It looks like a ghost town from an old Western. It was like the city was dead and just waiting for the rest of us to catch on.

"I hate this place," I muttered, pulling my sweatshirt neck up over my mouth, turtlelike.

"Don't blame you." Colin turned on his blinker for the dirt road that led down to the Barn. Even though there was no car to be seen and we hadn't passed another car since we left, Colin still stopped and looked both ways slowly. Someone must have gotten an A in driver's ed.

"I'm being serious."

"I wasn't doubting you." He looked over at me, his face

tinged slightly pink from the red dashboard lights. "What? I'm not yanking your chain."

"But you don't hate it here," I accused him.

"Why does it matter what I think?"

"Forget it." I looked out the window.

Colin pulled his truck off to the side of the road, the tires bouncing over the ruts left in the hardened mud from the last storm. Up ahead was the Barn. The Barn belongs to the McMurty family, but most of them moved away years ago. (Smart people, those McMurtys.) The widow McMurty, who judging by her appearance is approximately 259 years old, still lives in a house up near the highway, but no one has farmed the land for years. It was never clear to me why they hadn't just sold the place. Since she seems to be a zombie who never dies, things have stayed the way they were. My mom says that even when she was in high school, kids used to hang out at the Barn.

It's always referred to that way, the Barn, with a capital B. A stash of flashlights and lanterns is kept there, and people bring out coolers filled with ice and drinks. Almost always someone will have a portable radio that can be hooked up. Tonight the musical choice was a best of *American Idol* mix CD, which indicated that Darci Evers was somewhere on the premises. The Barn itself must have been built when things were designed to last. There are a few holes in some of the walls, and if you leaned against the stall dividers you would crash right through, but the floors are still solid, and if you don't have a fear of heights, the ladder to the hayloft will hold your weight. There's no heating, so hanging out at the Barn is a fair-weather activity, and this was the first weekend anyone had been out there.

Colin and I sat in the truck. The engine made ticking noises as it cooled down.

"Doesn't look like too many people are out here," I said, stating the obvious. There were only two other cars parked.

"It's cold. I suspect a bunch of people decided to skip it."

I gave an annoyed sigh. The whole night was a waste.

"Why are you pissed at me?" Colin asked.

"I'm not pissed." I uncrossed my arms and looked out the window. I could see a flashlight beam bouncing around inside.

"My parents own the farm. They expect me to live in Wheaton and take over."

"And that's what you want? To run a dairy farm?"

"Yeah." Colin shrugged.

"What about being an architect?"

"What are you talking about?"

"When we were kids you used to draw floor plans all the time of places you were going to build."

"I used to put on a cape and pretend I was Batman, too, but I wasn't considering that as a serious career move."

"You say you want to be a farmer because your dad is a farmer and his dad was a farmer. You'll marry someone from here and have tiny farmer children." I spit the last bit out as if his future children would be deformed freaks.

"Why do you care what I do?"

"Because you seem to have stopped caring! No one cares here. This entire town is a black hole of progress. The instant there's the tiniest shimmer of a new idea or a new way to do anything, it gets sucked down."

"You make it sound like we're out there plowing fields behind a horse."

"I'm not talking about farming! I'm talking about life. Life isn't supposed to be predictable. Take Darci Evers. She'll be queen of the spring dance for sure, she'll be voted Miss Community Service, she'll get married in her daddy's church as soon as possible to whoever in town has the most money, and she'll be head of the Wheaton Ladies' Society before you know it." I threw up my hands in disgust.

"Some people like knowing what's going to happen."

"You didn't used to. Now you're turning into someone who does exactly what's expected."

"You didn't expect me to kiss you," Colin said.

I felt my face flush red-hot. I pulled the sweatshirt neck up higher until it covered my nose. I could feel the steam of my breath filling the shirt.

"Yeah, well." I waved my hands vaguely in front of me like I was shooing something away.

"Yeah, well," he said. I could feel him looking at me, but I didn't look over.

The squeal of the barn door being yanked open cut off whatever he was about to say. Darci ran outside skipping, a can of beer held aloft in one hand. Justin, her long-term boyfriend, ran after her, and she squealed and ran just slow enough that he caught her in no time flat. He carried her back to the Barn and she pounded on his back with one tiny fist in mock indignation while making sure not to spill a drop of beer. Kimberly stood by the door, wavering back and forth.

"Now you put her down. Right now," Kimberly slurred, and then stumbled after them. A voice inside called for someone to close the door, the wind was cold.

"Great, Darci and Kimberly are here. And they brought a bunch of beer." I wasn't against drinking, but most of my classmates were not made any wittier by the infusion of alcohol. You have to wonder how Miss Jesus-Would-Just-Say-No preacher's daughter justified being such a hypocrite, but she never seemed to even notice.

"Don't you want to know why I kissed you? Or have you decided you know everything about here?"

I sucked my lower lip in and chewed on it, not saying a word.

"Emma?"

"I can predict Joann would never forgive me for sitting out here in the truck with you talking about this. I'm going to go in." I opened the door and jumped out.

I started walking toward the Barn, waiting to see if Colin was going to follow me. I couldn't decide if I wanted him to or not. Why did he have to pick this particular subject to be unpredictable on? I heard his door screech open and I stopped. He walked over with his hands shoved in his jeans pockets.

"What is this all about?" I asked. "Are you trying to prove a point, that I don't know everything?"

"No." He looked down and kicked at the ground. The earth was torn up by deep tire tracks in the mud that had dried into rock-hard, solid waves of dirt. "I would never want to do anything to hurt Joann," he added.

"Me either."

We stood, not looking at each other. It could have been a real teen dream kind of moment, except suddenly the sound of someone vomiting interrupted it. We looked over and saw Kimberly leaning against the Barn wall, heaving up her dinner and, if I had to guess, a few cans (or a case) of Miller Lite. Funny how you never saw beer advertisements ending like this.

"Eew, gross," Darci said, her head peeking out. She crossed her arms and watched Kimberly. I waited for her to look around and notice us, but with the lights and music coming from the barn, she must not have been able to see us standing off in the shadows.

"I really don't feel good," Kimberly muttered.

"What did you take?"

"I don't know, a whole bunch of stuff." Kimberly dry-heaved a few times. Even from here I could see that she must have been sweating. Her face looked oily in the moonlight. "I think I need to go to a doctor or something. My heart is beating all funny."

"Are you kidding me?" Darci screeched. "You can't go to the doctor. Your parents will find out and they'll tell my parents. How about we just take you home and you go to bed?"

"I don't know. Something's wrong."

"Don't be a fucking baby. How sick can you be? They advertise that stuff on the Internet. Do you want to get everyone into trouble?"

"No." Kimberly started to sniffle. It had the sound of full-blown waterworks on the rise. Darci stepped forward and rubbed Kimberly's back in slow circles.

"Sorry, I didn't mean to yell. I just meant if we got in trouble for drinking, we could get booted off the Spirit Squad! I know you don't want that. And your parents will ground you for sure from the spring dance, and Justin was just telling me inside that he thought Richard was going to ask you."

"Seriously?"

Darci crossed her heart with one pink fingernail.

"Totally seriously. Here, swish out your mouth with this water and take a Tic Tac." Darci handed over a plastic water bottle.

"I don't know."

"Do you want Richard to ask someone else?" Darci raised an eyebrow.

Kimberly spit the water on the ground, debating her options.

"Do you have any lip gloss?" she asked, holding out her hand for a mint. They wandered back inside.

"Let's get out of here," I whispered to Colin.

"You sure?"

"This is lame. I have a motto: 'Never join a party once the throwing up has started.'"

"Sounds wise." Colin swung back into his truck, and I plunked down on the seat next to him.

"Do you remember that game we played as kids?" I asked as we drove back to my place.

"Which one?"

"The one where one person goes 'My house . . .' and then the other person has to add to the sentence."

"Sort of. It wasn't much of a game."

"It was a great game. Let's do it. My house . . . is in Chicago . . ."

"And it's as large as a castle . . ."

"With a room just for my shoes . . . ," I added.

"Just one room?" he asked with a snort. I jabbed him in the side.

"You're not playing right. With a room for my shoes . . ."

"And a room to watch football with a fifty-inch high-def TV . . . ," Colin said.

"Fifty-inch? Overkill . . . okay, and my house has a pool and a track around the roof . . ."

"That I designed . . ."

"See! I knew you still wanted to be an architect. Farmer, my ass," I said.

"Now *you're* not playing," he interrupted.

"Okay, that I designed myself . . . winning major awards . . . ," I said to encourage him.

"Which I put next to my Olympic gold medals I won for track and field . . ."

I gave a hoot of appreciation. We played the rest of the way home until Colin pulled to a stop just down the road from my house. He clicked off the lights. My real house was dark; Mom must have gone to bed. I reached over to open the door when Colin grabbed my arm. I spun around as if he had grabbed my nonexistent boobs instead of just my arm. He dropped his hand immediately.

"Hang on a minute."

I sat back, but he didn't say anything else. He put his hands on the ten and two of the steering wheel as if he was getting ready for a particularly tricky maneuver on the driver's ed test.

"I've wanted to talk to you," he said finally.

"So talk."

"About what happened at Christmas."

"Look, don't worry about it. It was some kind of freakish mistake."

"That's the thing, it wasn't a mistake. I mean, it wasn't like I had a plan, but it wasn't a mistake."

All the air seemed to be sucked out of the truck cab. I couldn't take a deep breath, and I noticed that my hands were shaking, so I sat on them. I wasn't sure exactly what I was supposed to say. This was Colin, for crying out loud. We had watched *Sesame Street* together. He was the closest thing I had to family other than my mom. He was my best friend's boyfriend.

"I like you," he said.

My heart was speeding up.

"I like you, too."

"I mean, I think I really like you." Colin was moving closer. I could smell the detergent his mother used on his clothes, and over that, the smell of freshly dug earth. He must have been working on the farm after school.

"What about Joann?" I said in a whisper, as if someone might overhear us. As if she was going to pop up from the backseat and yell surprise before bursting into tears.

"I don't know."

"What the hell, Colin?" Part of me desperately wanted him to shut up and never say another word about this, and another part of me, a part I didn't like so much, wanted him to keep talking.

"I don't know. I'm not trying to piss you off, but I feel that I have to say something. I've liked you for as long as I can remember. I liked you since before I fully understood what it meant, but you were always so clear about wanting to be friends, just friends, that I never said a thing. Heck, I half convinced myself that I didn't care. That I was fine with that. Besides, even if you liked me, I knew the relationship wouldn't go anywhere. You've talked about leaving since you understood there was a road out of town. But I think I never stopped liking you. I felt like you should know. Then I kissed you, and you kissed me back." Colin looked over at me. "You did kiss me back."

"What did you expect me to do? Run screaming?"

Colin shook his head and looked back out the window.

"You kissed me back. Like you had been waiting for me to kiss you."

I didn't say anything. Instead I focused on pulling a loose string from the cuff of my shirt. I wondered if it was a key string, the one that was holding everything together, and maybe if I pulled it too hard, my whole shirt would unravel.

"Look, Colin, it's complicated."

"But you're not saying no."

"Joann's my best friend," I said, finally reminding him and myself at the same time.

"If I weren't dating her, would you go out with me?"

"I don't know. Does it matter? You *are* going out with her."

"What if we're meant to be together?" he asked.

"Then I guess none of this would have happened."

"But it did. And you kissed me. And then here we are, so the question is, what do we do now?"

I could feel my heart pounding, and I couldn't look at Colin. I fully expected a bolt of lightning to come out of the sky and take us out in the truck. If God had more room on those stone tablets, I'm pretty sure the Eleventh Commandment would have been "Thou shalt not betray thine best friend with her boyfriend—even if he is hot." Colin reached his hand over; his finger ran down my arm. Every hair on my arm stood straight up as if wanting to meet his touch. I yanked my arm back, cracking my elbow on the truck door. The feeling racing through me was not one that you had for a brother, or a best friend's boyfriend.

"Guess that's my answer, huh?" Colin said, pulling back over to his side of the truck.

"You're one of my best friends."

"The famous 'let's just be friends' talk, huh?" Colin said, trying to make it sound like a joke, but I could tell it wasn't.

I jumped down out of the truck and then leaned back in.

"I'm thinking we shouldn't tell Joann about this."

"About what?"

"Tonight," I said, wondering if he was trying to be annoying or if it just came naturally.

"What about it?"

"Are you trying to piss me off?"

"Maybe." He gave me a smile, and I felt my stomach do a slow turnover. "Anything else we shouldn't tell her?" he asked.

My heart pounded, and I had the feeling he was going to kiss me again. Part of me wanted to slam the door shut, and the other part wanted to lunge across the seat and kiss him first. I waited for God to strike me dead.

What would Jesus do? I mean, what would Jesus do if he were the kind of guy to consider kissing his best friend's girlfriend? Why doesn't the Bible cover these kinds of situations?

"Nope," I squeaked, and then cleared my throat. "Nothing else."

"I'll make sure you get back in safe."

"In case the Boston Strangler took a serious wrong turn and is lying in wait for me?" I asked. Wheaton was not exactly a hotbed of crime. One time a bunch of junior high kids stole the plywood cutouts the Hansens keep on their lawn of a fat lady bending over showing off her bloomers. It rated the front page of the paper; it was that big of a deal.

Colin shrugged. He was going to wait anyway. He had that sort of John Wayne–type sense of nobility. I gave Colin another look and then jogged back to my house. I turned back, but I couldn't see anything in the dark expect the outline of his truck. I slid the window open and hoisted myself up. Once I was in, I saw Colin flash his headlights and heard the engine start up. I could hear the sound of a siren in the distance. Maybe the cops were on the tail of the Strangler after all.

8

God, is it so bad to want something that you know is wrong? I mean, I know it's bad, but is it bad *bad? Damned to hell kind of bad, or the kind of bad where if I feel really sorry about it later all can be forgiven? On a bad scale, where one is having a nasty thought and ten is setting kittens on fire, where does this fall? Is there a special level of hell for those who screw over a friend?*

I lay on my bed staring up at Johnny. I couldn't sleep. The only way I could tell time was moving forward was by counting the times I heard the fridge fan motor kick on. I punched my pillow in an effort to fluff it and tried not to think how tired I was going to be at the track meet in the morning. It wasn't a regional, but I still wanted killer times. Who knew how Northwestern was going to make their final decision? I pulled the blankets up and rolled back onto my side, curling up around Mr. Muffles. The whole thing was stupid. There was no reason to be thinking about it at all. Colin felt the need to ask, and I gave a clear answer. Now if I could only convince myself that I didn't want to go running after his truck screaming, "Do-over!"

I tried to sort out what I was feeling. It shouldn't have been that hard, because when you stripped away all the fluff, it really came down to two options:

1. I didn't like Colin.
2. I did like Colin.

Given only two options, it shouldn't have seemed so complicated, and at the same time, it was. I can't remember a time I haven't known Colin, and although I hated that everyone was always trying to fix us up, I think I had assumed we would go out at some point. There is no doubt Colin is good-looking. He has a sort of Zac Efron, guy-next-door thing going on. Then there's the fact that all the work on his parents' farm, plus football, has given him a pretty darn nice body. Not that I've spent a lot of time checking him out, but a girl can tell. Colin is smart, and his idea of humor doesn't rely on fart jokes. I liked that about him. I liked that he could make me laugh, and how we could be together and not talk about anything and still have a good time. I never wanted to risk our friendship with mucking things up, but in the end I guess he felt that he belonged to me. That he was mine.

Then there were all the reasons not to like Colin (separate from the whole ruining-my-life aspect of him dating my best friend). Colin loved Wheaton. Sure, he might act like it bugged him once in a while, and it's possible it did bug him, but in the end this was home. Colin would hate Chicago, and I would hate staying here, so it left us in this position where we didn't want the same things at all. Colin hadn't even bothered applying to any college. He figured he'd just take a few classes at one of the community colleges. Not as a fallback safety plan, but as his main plan. Granted, I had no plan B if the scholarship at Northwestern didn't work out, but at least my plan was ambitious. Who has the community college that accepts anyone as their plan? Was having a good time with someone right now the same as wanting to be with that person sometime later? Where would we go from here? High school would be over in a few months. What then? What's the point? To say that we did? To see what would happen, when we sort of know what would happen?

I could argue that there was no reason to like Colin at all, just fond memories of an old friend. An old friend who just happens to be hot. Friends can be hot, but it doesn't mean that you have to act on it, that it causes you to feel anything. The problem was, I couldn't argue with the fact that I felt something.

I rolled over. Even if I could sort out how I felt, then there was the issue of how Joann would respond to this revelation. If I told Joann that Colin and I were destined to be together and that we were going to be a couple, there were a few ways she could respond:

1. She could be angry.
2. She could be understanding.
3. She could reach a new level of rage in which her eyes shot fire and she raised the town locals up against me and they would come for me, ready to stone me alive.

I wondered what Colin would do. Would he break up with Joann regardless of what I decided? Would he tell her he harbored these feelings for me? What if he had already told her? What was that going to do to Joann? Colin was her first real boyfriend, as I don't think we can count Barry, who used to push her down and kiss her when we were in fourth grade. Playground violence does not a relationship make, even on the Jerry Springer show. I rolled over again.

Was Colin lying at home tossing and turning too, or was he doing the guy thing and not even noticing at all?

Lastly, even if I sorted out how I felt and survived the fire from Joann's eyes, there was still the fact I would have to live with myself, and I wasn't sure I could do that. Which brought me pretty much back around to where I started. Liking him, not liking him, and not able to really do either very well.

9

God, here's a question for you: There are winners and losers, and I'm pretty much betting everyone is praying to be the winner, so how do you decide whose prayer to grant? You can't fool me that it's always the most deserving, so there must be some other criteria. Not that I'm trying to imply you can be bought off, but if there was something that made you more inclined to favor one prayer over another, I would be open to hearing about it.

Someday when I appear on the *Today* show to talk to Matt Lauer about my Olympic win, I will have one nice thing to say about Wheaton: It's where I learned to run. Wheaton has no public transportation—unless you count Mr. Kundert, who drives his tractor *everywhere* and will pick you up if you're walking by the side of the road. If you don't want to wait for the tractor train, then you have to either rely on your parents to give you a ride, own a bike, or get your own car. Or you hoof it.

1. Parents: As I have already detailed, I do not have parents, I have only the singular parent. One who works long hours and "can't be cruising around like some kind of Greyhound bus driver."
2. Bike: Wheaton isn't exactly a Tour de France kind of town. For some reason, once you outgrow either your BMX or banana seat roadster with the tassels on the handlebars, no one bikes. I'm not even sure they sell adult bikes in town. If Lance Armstrong came to town, everyone would wonder why he was wearing those funny tight pants.
3. Own a car: This requires funds or generous parent(s). I have no money to buy a car. As for generous parent(s), see point one above.
4. Hoof it: I walked to get everywhere, and eventually I wanted to get there quicker, so I started running. The rest, as they say, is history.

The track meet was in Van Wert. I stood near the blocks, shaking my legs and ignoring everyone else. Track is one part speed, one part guts, and one part psychology.

You need to focus before a race. Find your inner Zen kind of thing. Visualize yourself crossing the finish line way out in front of everyone else. The girl on my left apparently didn't get the memo, because she kept blathering on. It was like she had Tourette's and was incapable of shutting up.

"I love your shoes! They match our uniforms. Isn't that funny, I mean that they would match our uniforms versus yours? Are they Nikes? I love Nike. I think it's the swoosh. I tell myself I'm going to swoosh." She giggled.

I looked over. She wore her hair in pigtails. Pigtails. It's debatable if one should ever wear pigtails over the age of seven, but certainly not to a track meet. Do you see serious athletes wearing pigtails? I rest my case.

"Is my number on straight? I can't tell." She picked at the pins that held her number to her chest.

"It doesn't matter," I said.

"Huh?"

I placed my foot in the blocks and took a deep breath. I shook my head, trying to clear the fog out of my brain. I was tired and could feel a headache starting from the lack of sleep. Thanks, Colin.

"It doesn't matter if your number is on straight, because I won't be able to see it." I shot her a look with a smile. "I'll be in front of you the whole way."

"READY?" The call came out over the PA system. I felt my heart slow down and my vision narrow. I pulled in deep, slow breaths. I could smell the cut grass from the soccer field next door. I kept my eyes on the track ahead of me. I could hear a hum, which would have been Pigtails chattering, but I wasn't focused on her anymore.

The starter pistol went off, and I shot out of the blocks. I could feel everything slide past me. I had been training this year with ankle and wrist weights, so when I ran without them during the meets I felt lighter than air. The only thing I could hear was my heart and the sound of my shoes (Asics, by the way—they kick Nike ass) hitting the track and pushing me forward. On the final corner I could see a flash of color out of the corner of my eye. Someone was really piling it on. My breath was ragged and my legs felt heavy. I closed my eyes for just an instant and pictured Chicago in front of me and Wheaton behind me. My legs found the extra steam and pushed through the last few meters. I heard the whistles and cheers, but I couldn't tell who won. I slowed down and walked bent over, sucking in deep breaths. I could see Pigtails cross the line last. I was right; her number didn't matter. I looked up to see Coach Attley punching the air with a victory fist. Looked like a win. I let myself break into a smile.

"PROCTOR!"

I yanked my head around to see who was cheering for me. No one comes to my track meets. Fair enough, watching people run around in a circle isn't the most exciting thing. My mom sometimes comes to the big regional meets, but otherwise my only cheering section was the other members of the track team. The rest of the student body at TES couldn't be bothered. As far as they were concerned there were only two sports: basketball and football. Track was what people did to stay in shape for other sports or to have something to list on their college apps. I was the only one who took it seriously.

Colin was standing by the fence. He gave a wave. Colin was here. Colin was at my meet. Even though the race was over, my heart sped up again, and I felt myself give a huge smile. Was this a sign? Maybe sometimes you have to take a risk without worrying about the potential disaster. I shouldn't assume things have to go badly. We needed to talk. I saw a few people jostling for position around the fence line. Was it?

It was.

Joann had woven her way through the crowd to Colin. They stood together, waving and cheering. They were waving so wildly it looked like they were trying to flag down low-flying aircraft. The smile dropped off my face. I waved but didn't go over right away. I went over to our bench and grabbed my water bottle and warm-up gear. I needed a second. By the time I jogged back, they were already standing at the gate. Holding hands. Not that it mattered.

"Did you hear?" Joann asked as soon as I got close.

"Hear what?" I looked back and forth between the two of them. Colin wouldn't meet my eyes, but he threw his arm around Joann as if staking a claim. My chest felt tight again, as if I still hadn't gotten my breath back.

"Kimberly Ryan is in the hospital. She was staying the night at Darci's house, and apparently she had some kind of seizure or something," said Joann, her eyes wide. "Everyone is freaking out."

I opened my mouth to give my opinion that there was nothing wrong with Kimberly that a few hours of sobriety wouldn't cure, when Colin caught my eye, shaking his head slightly. Right. If I wasn't at the Barn last night, then I didn't see anything. I swallowed down my comment. Joann's face was flushed; she was loving the drama. Nothing a small town likes better then drama.

"Wow," I mumbled, at a loss to say anything of any use.

"She still hasn't come around. Reverend Evers is planning a prayer meeting at the church for her, and everybody is going."

"Why bother with modern medicine when you've got the power of prayer on your side?" I said. Joann pulled back as if I had slapped her. I could feel my headache coming back.

"They're asking for all of her friends to be there," Colin added.

"We aren't really friends," I said.

"At a time like this, all of us are friends," Joann said. She saw my expression. "I know she can be a pain, but this could be serious. Healthy girls don't just pass out and not wake up."

"Yeah. It's a mystery, all right." I watched Colin; he looked straight at me with his chin thrust out.

Joann was gesturing to Colin's truck and didn't notice. "We're driving into Fort Wayne to pick up a lunch meat tray and sheet cake from the Meijer's to take over to the hospital."

There's a long-standing belief in small towns that there is very little that can't be made better by a potluck. Funerals, weddings, Girl Scout meetings, you name it, add a spiral honey-baked ham and you've got a party. If people were buying food in bulk, then it truly was a serious event.

"We came down to get you so we could go together," Joann said.

I pictured myself sitting in the truck sandwiched between the two of them. It was enough to put a girl off her processed lunch meat.

"I have to wait until the end for the medals. I won my race."

"Do you have to?" she asked, disappointment in her voice. I'm sure both of them were on the verge of congratulating me on my big win, except for the more pressing need to rush to the side of someone they didn't even like that much. Both of them knew how much track mattered to me, and neither of them could work themselves up to express even the slightest interest. Hell, they didn't have to really *be* interested, but would it be asking too much for them to *act* interested? I certainly did plenty of acting in our relationships; you'd think they could return the favor.

"I should go back with the rest of the team." I shrugged and wiped the sweat off my face. I'll bet I smelled foul. Joann and Colin both looked perfect, like some kind of ad for wholesome teens. If you were playing the game of which one of these things doesn't belong, you could have a massive brain injury and still pick me out of the lineup as the odd one out. I couldn't believe I gave up sleep for this. What the hell had I been thinking?

"You sure? We could wait if you need to stay a bit longer," Joann offered.

"No, you guys better go. You don't want to hold up the sheet cake."

"You okay? You seem upset."

"Yeah, what's the problem? You won, didn't you?" Colin added, his voice leaning toward bitterness.

"I'm the winner, all right." I turned away from both of them and looked back at the track team. "I'm fine, just focused."

"Well, maybe we should go before we distract you, huh?" Colin said.

"I'll catch up with you later," I said, fighting the urge to stick my tongue out at him.

I watched them for a minute as they went back to the truck. Joann was keyed up from all the drama and excitement. She was practically skipping; the only thing that kept her tethered to the ground was Colin's hand. They made a great couple.

10

God, are you still paying attention? In fairness, I got bored with Lost *after the first season, and 24 got weird after a few years too. There are only so many nuclear bombs that can go off before you start thinking there has to be something more upbeat to watch. And don't even get me started on* America's Next Top Model. *After season three, even Tyra's hair extensions look tired. So I figure if I get bored with a show after a few years, you must get sick of keeping an eye on everything down here. A few millennia of watching* Earth: The World's Only Real Reality TV*—it's understandable that you're sick of it. However, and don't take this as a criticism, it is kind of your job, and if I'm not mistaken, lately it seems like you haven't had your eye on the ball. You might want to tune in.*

I used to love watching cartoons. Sometimes they would show a tiny, itsy-bitsy snowflake falling onto the top of a big hill, and it would begin to roll down, becoming a tiny snowball, gathering speed along the way, and by the time it got to the end it would be a snowball the size of a house, consuming everything in its path. The situation with Kimberly was like that.

Kimberly regained consciousness but couldn't (apparently) recall anything about what had happened. The doctors declared that her problem had been "drug related." They might as well have come out and said her problem was that she was kidnapped and probed by aliens. People were shocked. Kimberly was a "good girl." Her dad was the chief of police and her mom volunteered at the church—being good was in her genetic makeup. Then there was the fact that she was best friends with Darci, everyone's favorite hypocrite. In Wheaton good girl versus bad girl status was established in elementary school. Changing sides rarely happened, no matter what reality might lead you to believe.

If Kimberly had drugs in her system, then the question remained, how did they get there?

a. Kim took the drugs on purpose.
(A good girl like her? Never.)

b. Kim took the drugs by accident.
(Perhaps she tripped and they fell into her mouth.)

c. Kim was slipped the drugs by some evil, nefarious

person who clearly intended to harm her while she was engaged in some innocent activity, like knitting socks for orphans in some cesspool of a Third World country.

Only in Wheaton would (c) be chosen as the answer. Darci and Kimberly maintained they were at Darci's house all night, having an innocent sleepover. They would tell this story with wide, blinking eyes, their hands folded under their chins. If the preacher's daughter says she was home, then she was home.

Going to church in Wheaton is a mandatory activity. There is no obvious attendance taking—it isn't like Reverend Evers calls off roll at the start of service—but mark my words, everyone is aware of who's there and who isn't. You'd have to have a major organ falling out before you would be excused from service. Even then they would encourage you to drag yourself in (perhaps holding your liver in a plastic shopping bag) and be prayed over before returning to the hospital. Sometimes Joann and I sat next to each other in the back, where we would be free to whisper about the seemingly direct relationship between faith and big hair. Reverend Evers's wife seemed to style her hair taller each week, as if trying to be closer to God.

Today when I came in I noticed that Joann and Colin were sitting together, sandwiched between their families. Their mothers looked like they might be swapping Crock-Pot recipes while their dads talked over the Colts' chances to make the Superbowl. Joann waved me over to join them, but I couldn't imagine squishing into the pew. It was clear to me there wasn't any room.

You would think if they wanted you to attend church, they would make it a welcoming place, but the pews at Trinity Evangelical were carved from some type of hard wood designed for maximum discomfort. I shifted again; I was stiff from the meet yesterday. My mother shot me a look indicating I should sit still. I swallowed a sigh. This is why we don't usually sit near each other. Reverend Evers was on a rant. He had that little white spit blob in the corner of his mouth, and he was gripping the pulpit like a man going down for the last time. I snuck a look at my watch.

"Make no mistake, the devil is among us. He's on the radio singing along with the hip-hop. He's on the TV and in the godless movies that come out of Hollywood. He's in our children's books, which glorify witchcraft."

Reverend Evers has a serious hatred for Harry Potter. In his opinion, the boy wizard might as well grow horns. He takes the success of the books as a personal affront. He can't understand their popularity. Not that he's ever read any of the books, mind you, but apparently he could tell by the covers that they weren't worth the paper they were written on. So much for the "don't judge a book by its cover" theory. Reverend Evers tried to schedule a book burning after the last book came out, but only three people showed up. Three books on fire looks less like a political statement and more like a small barbecue.

"We have seen ourselves as safe. We have built a community based on God, but the devil creeps in even here. Now our children are at risk. The devil is coming for our babies!" Preacher Evers rumbled.

A few of the small kids peered around, looking a little fearful. The adults were nodding. I couldn't look over—if Joann and Colin were nodding too, I would have to run screaming from the church. Kimberly's parents were in the first row, with Kimberly between them. She looked pale, but otherwise fine. Darci sang in the choir along with her mother, and if I wasn't mistaken, she had on a touch of glitter lip gloss and her hair looked shellacked. She was in tall hair training.

"Someone has come into our community and tried to take one of our own, to poison her. I say we will be a voice in the darkness crying out NO MORE! We will create a wall of unity that shall protect our families and keep out those who would harm us. Linked arms and linked hearts. We will keep our children safe in the arms of the Lord, as Mark 10:14 tells us, "Suffer the little children to come unto me, and forbid them not: for of such is the kingdom of God." Today we give thanks that our little lamb Kimberly has been returned safely to us. We thank God for listening to our prayers, and we vow here today as a community to ferret out those who did this. We will not rest until we have thrown the devil out of our town!"

Reverend Evers dropped his head. I had the sense he was waiting for applause. I was terrified it was going to be like a horror movie and he would bop back up and keep going. He was the Jason of preachers, but instead of a chain saw, he wielded a Bible and a serious case of judgment. Thankfully, he seemed done. We were in the home stretch. A couple of prayers, a song, and we would be out. I really needed him to wrap it up. I still hadn't done my paper for English class on *A Tale of Two Cities*.

That's when it happened.

Darci gave a small cry and tumbled off the choir riser. She slumped to the floor. She lay still for a second and then began to shake and shudder. It appeared to be a very stylish seizure. Everyone stood up at once, as if we were planning to break into a round of "Amazing Grace." Darci's mom and dad ran to her side and dropped to the floor next to her. There was no sound for a split second; it was absolutely silent in the church, as if everyone was waiting for the sound waves to ripple out of the room.

"Someone call 911!" a voice yelled out, and then everyone began to panic. Kids cried, and there was a crash as someone dropped her purse, its contents clattering down on the tile floor. Some people pushed up toward the action, while others tried to start herding their families out of the church. A few more stood in place, as if they weren't sure if they were coming or going.

I think it was safe to say church service was officially over.

11

God, you know the Bible story about the tower of Babel, where no one can understand anyone else? Sometimes I think I'm living out that story. Everyone around me is speaking English, but we don't understand one another at all. I have to tell you, if I were going to pick a Bible story to live out, this wouldn't be it. I would prefer to be in the garden with a cute Adam (no fig leaf required). No disrespect to Eve, of course. To be honest, I would prefer Noah's ark, even with the catastrophic flood aspect. I like animals. In fact, I like animals more than I like most people I know. Then again, if I have to live out a Bible story, the Babel story is better than most of Revelation. The horsemen of the apocalypse freak me out.

"You have to help me with this. I've got to send it in next week and I have nothing." I looked down at the computer screen in disgust. The curser blinked, and I'm fairly sure it was blinking in Morse code, "*You're an idiot, you're an idiot.*" Every time a letter from Northwestern came in the mail my heart would speed up, and every time it was a demand for something else. You ask people for a few zillion dollars so you can go to their school, and they keep demanding things of you. I wished they would just let me know if I had the scholarship or if I was going to have to sell off a kidney to go there, because there was no way I was staying here. I looked at the letter again and wondered if instead of answering the question I could just send in a copy of the results from the meet that weekend.

"What part are you stuck on?" Joann asked.

I doubted she was taking my crisis seriously, since she wasn't even looking up from *Vogue*. Of course, in fairness, I hadn't told her about not applying anywhere else either, so it's possible she didn't grasp the severity of the situation. She held up a page of the magazine to me.

"Do you think I would look fat in this?"

"Everyone would look fat in that," I said.

"Huh." She scrunched her eyes up at it. "Keira Knightley doesn't look fat in it."

"Keira Knightley is a human hanger. I suspect she considers a single grain of rice to be a well-rounded meal."

"I still like the pants, plus Colin loves Keira."

"You realize, of course, that while you're debating the

pros and cons of the wisdom of high-waisted sailor pants, my future hangs in the balance?"

"Okay, sorry. I'm paying attention." She put down the magazine.

"This scholarship application has this stupid essay requirement."

"What's the matter with those snooty colleges? It's like they want you to be capable of thought in order to go to their fancy school. It sounds discriminatory to me."

I started to nod in agreement when I realized that she was making fun of me.

"Your wit is not appreciated."

Joann tossed a pillow at my head with a laugh.

"You're good in English. What's the problem?"

"How are you supposed to answer a question like 'Why have you chosen Northwestern University and what do you hope to get from your educational experience?' How am I supposed to know what I want to get? You just know the correct answer is not the truth." I mimed typing on the computer. "Dear Admissions Officer, by attending your fine ivory tower of higher learning I hope to get as far away from my hometown as possible."

"You need to put stuff like, 'Through athletics I have learned the importance of preparation and effort, and I hope to transfer these skills to the world of academics and win the most important race: life.'"

I looked over at her with my mouth open. I had no idea Joann was capable of such huge volumes of BS. You think you know people.

"That was so good. Scary good. Hang on, I want to write that down before I forget." I started typing feverishly on the computer.

"With everything going on, I bet you won't be the only one thinking about going away to school now."

"What are you talking about?"

"The poisonings?" Joann sat there looking at me, as if she suspected I had a head injury. "Didn't you hear? They got Kelly, too."

Joann looked out the window, as if she expected someone to be sneaking up on her from behind. I tried not to roll my eyes.

"Now Kelly is sick?"

"Uh-huh. It happened at the Spirit Squad! meeting after school. They were making a big get-well poster for Darci and apparently, all of a sudden, she told people she was feeling funny, lightheaded, and then *wham*, she fell over." Joann snapped her fingers. "Just like that. Cut down in her prime."

"I bet Darci is not too happy to share the spotlight even more."

"What are you talking about?"

"Don't you find it the tiniest bit odd that Darci sees Kimberly getting all this attention and then suddenly she has the same problem?"

"Darci and Kimberly are best friends. It isn't like they have some big competition."

I shrugged and looked back at the computer screen.

"No matter what you think of Darci, someone slipped something to Kimberly. Something happened, and someone made it happen. The hospital is running all kinds of tests on the three of them to see if they can figure out any common factors."

"There were no drugs in Darci's system. Zero. I'm willing to bet there wasn't anything in Kelly's system either. You want to know the common factor? The desire for attention."

"You can't think they would fake something this serious."

"They're some of the most annoying girls at school, but honestly, who would actually poison them?"

"My mom said she saw the Evers family down at the Stop and Shop, and they think it might be terrorists."

"Terrorists? Please tell me you're joking."

Joann's face was serious. No joke. I turned off the computer.

"Why would terrorists poison three girls in Middle of Nowhere, Indiana?"

"Not middle of nowhere. America's heartland." Joann paused to let that sink in. "Plus, all the girls go to a Christian school. Reverend Evers told my mom by attacking here they create a culture of fear, which is exactly what they do. Terrorize."

"This is Wheaton. If you pierce your ears, you can't walk a block without at least four people noticing and calling your parents to see if they know. Can you actually imagine that some terrorist is going to slink into town with a bag of drugs and not be noticed?"

"But that's the thing. Mrs. Homer told the police that she saw a car with suspicious people on Friday night. They were driving without their headlights, and she thinks she heard that weird Middle Eastern music coming from the car."

"Mrs. Homer is, like, a hundred and ten years old. She can't recognize her own family members if they're standing right in front of her, screaming their names. She makes Helen Keller look like an eagle eye. This is the person we're trusting to spot Osama?"

"She didn't say she saw their faces. Just that they were, you know, brown."

"Brown? Well then, they must be guilty of something. Imagine that, being brown. You think they would have known they would stick out here in the whitest town in America. Although I suppose since they're brown, we shouldn't expect them to be too smart."

"What is the matter with you? It's like you're taking their side." Joann's face was flushed. "The town is pulling together over this. Didn't you hear Reverend Evers? We need to stand together. I know you don't like Darci, but I wouldn't think you were mean enough to want someone to hurt her."

"No one hurt her. I'm not taking sides, because there isn't a side."

"Then what happened to them?"

"I don't think anything happened to Darci."

"And Kimberly? How do you explain what happened to her?"

I chewed on the inside of my lip, frustrated that I couldn't say more.

"Look, you know Kimberly. Do you really think she's the kind who wouldn't take drugs? What about the time at the Barn last year when she had all those wine coolers and ended up passing out in the horse stall and no one could find her for, like, an hour? Or when she got it in her head that she'd take all those diet pills to lose weight and ended up throwing up in gym class? She spewed right through the volleyball net. She might convince her parents she's an angel, but you know she's not."

"But she was at Darci's that night. No way they would do anything like that at Reverend Evers's house. Even Kimberly would never take that kind of chance. Getting wasted at his house. I don't think so."

"Maybe they weren't there. They could sneak out. Darci's bedroom is on the first floor," I said. Joann raised one eyebrow in doubt. "What? You think it's more likely that Al-Qaeda crawled in her window than that she crawled out?"

"Whatever." Joann picked up the magazine and flipped through it, slapping the pages over more loudly than necessary.

I sat with my legs crossed, my leg bouncing up and down, watching her. She didn't look at me, so I spun back around to the computer and jabbed the on button, then jammed it off again and turned back.

"Why are you so excited about the whole thing?" I asked her.

"What?"

"You and everyone else are all in a lather. It's all anyone is talking about."

"Uh, hello, it's a huge deal."

"No, it's not. Everyone has made it into a big deal. There are things they could be worried about that matter. No one cares what happens twenty minutes outside of this town. People care more about corn prices than they do about the war, or the environment, or debt reduction in the Third World. It's pathetic. There's plenty of drama in the world without having to make up our own."

"Oh, spare me your Bono imitation." Joann stood and tossed the *Vogue* down on the sofa. She jammed her feet into her shoes. "You are so busy proving that you're above us all that you don't even care what happens right in front of you. Better polish up your saddle for your high horse before you gallop out of town."

"High horse? What, because I want to do better than Wheaton?"

"No, because you imply that anyone who wants to stay here is a loser. That we've settled. How do you think that makes me feel?" Joann's eyes filled with tears.

"Joann," I said.

"You know what? Don't start. Don't even start. Whatever you say now doesn't matter. You've made your point over and over. This town sucks. Anyone who lives here is stuck in a time warp, and anyone who likes it here must be a backward hick. So you know what? Fill out your applications, run your races, win yourself a fancy scholarship, and then you can move away and make friends with more interesting people."

Joann stomped out of the room and slammed the front door on her way out. I sat there not moving for a minute, and then I attacked the *Vogue* magazine. I tore pages out, yanking them by the handful, shredding them and hurling them to the floor. I was crying, deep, choking wails, with snot smeared under my nose. Only when there was nothing more than colored confetti all over the floor did I stop. I picked up a piece and saw Keira Knightley staring back at me, and then I started crying all over again.

12

God, about the Bible . . . I know it's supposed to be your word and a lot of it is pretty good (although there are a few parts where the pacing drags; between you and me, you could have cut some of those so-and-so begat so-and-so sections and just stuck those in the back in an appendix or something). What I'm wondering is if there isn't a chance that a few of your scribes got some sections wrong? My mom can't take a phone message without screwing it up, so I'm just saying you might want to take a look over a few of the sections and see if that's what you really wanted to say. Plus, there are parts where you totally contradict yourself. For example, is it an eye for an eye or turn the other cheek? Not that a person can't say two completely different things and mean both of them in the moment. I'm living proof, a walking contradiction—but I think we all expect more of you, being a deity and all.

Joann and I became best friends in first grade. Being that I was an only child, I was still in the process of learning the fine art of sharing. Joann had come to school with every possible school supply one could want. Her parents had outfitted her for elementary school with the kind of care and precision nations spend on military troops. There would be no occasion that would arise where Joann would be without the proper writing or art implement.

I sat at my desk with my sleeves pulled up over my hands. They washed the desks with some kind of oily cleanser. It smelled off, like yogurt pushed to the back of the fridge and forgotten. I didn't mind if it got on my sweater, as I was hoping that I would have a chance to get a new one. We were supposed to be drawing pictures of our families. Maybe it was because I only had to draw my mom and me, or the fact that I had zero artistic talent, but I was done while everyone else still seemed to be busy.

Joann sat next to me. Her hair was pulled back in a tight ponytail; it was a wonder she could blink. Her school uniform was clearly brand-new; the pleats were razor sharp, and I swear you could have grated cheese on them. My mom had bought my uniforms at the school swap during the summer. The colors on my skirt were washed out, and the pleats, instead of firm, straight lines like those on my notebook paper, were limp waves. Joann's crayons were new, each one with a sharp point. Everything about her looked clean, shiny, and new. I looked down at my crayons. We hadn't bought a new box. My mom pointed out that I had plenty of crayons already and had gathered an odd assortment and put them in a Tupperware container. It seemed okay at the time, but it was clear now that it was anything but okay.

It was then that I got the idea to draw in a father. I was too young to know the term "artistic license," but I understood the concept. This was my drawing, and if I wanted a father, I would simply make myself one. A friendly, Mr. Brady kind of dad. This would require brown. A nice, stable-looking brown. I looked down at my crayons; the brown was already worn down, the paper torn off. It seemed a shabby brown for such a noble man. I shot another glance over at Joann. On her desk there were no less than three shades of brown.

I wanted those crayons.

I needed those crayons.

That morning we had covered the Ten Commandments in class. Suddenly the meaning of number ten, about coveting your neighbor's goods, was making a whole lot of sense. Given that I was already violating one of the commandments, it seemed like I might as well take on another. I was seriously considering breaking number seven (thou shalt not steal) and swiping one of her crayons.

I waited for just the right moment. Joann had the tip of her tongue poking out between her teeth as she colored. I leaned into the aisle, closer and closer. She didn't notice. She pressed her crayon to the paper, making a sun to hang in the sky over her family. Right at that moment I slipped a crayon off the side of her desk into my pocket. She didn't notice. I looked down carefully. I had managed to snatch burnt sienna. I stroked the smooth wax tube. I liked the place where the paper met the wax. That's when Darci let out her wail.

"She stole a crayon!" Darci stood at her desk, pointing an accusatory finger in my direction. The class turned to face me.

"Emma? Have you taken something that doesn't belong to you?" our teacher asked, her voice firm. Darci was nodding madly, a pint-size advocate of the death penalty. I didn't know what they would do to me, but I knew I was in trouble. My first day and I had already blown it. My throat tightened, and I held the crayon in my fist, wishing it would disappear.

"She didn't steal the crayon. I told her she could have it," Joann said.

She went back to her drawing, and the rest of the class continued without another word on the subject. At recess I handed Joann the crayon shyly.

"I'm sorry," I whispered.

"I have lots of crayons."

That was the end of the discussion and the beginning of our friendship. I always thought it was interesting that we knew the exact moment we became friends. I had never really thought about the end. I assumed we would be friends forever.

I wondered if the fact that we had been friends for so long would be enough to keep us friends when we had less in common. It was somehow different from my relationship with Colin. That was all about us being opposites. My friendship with Joann was about shared things. If we didn't have those, then I wasn't sure what would tie us together, but it didn't mean I didn't still want to have her in my life. Joann was wrong when she said I thought less of her for wanting to stay in Wheaton. I didn't get why she'd want to, but I didn't think less of her. It was important that we stay friends. Not having her in my life would be like cutting off everything that had happened. Having her around was proof.

➡ ➡ ➡

I wove my way through the halls looking for Joann the morning after our fight. I'd called her last night, but her mother told me in a frosty voice, "As it's after nine p.m., Joann will not be taking calls." Sometimes reaching Joann is like trying to call the Queen of England.

Everyone was in tight clusters, discussing the three "poisonings" and talking in hushed voices about the terrorist threat. I avoided getting sucked into any of the conversations. I would find it impossible to avoid screaming, "BROWN PERSON" just so I could watch them drop to the floor in terror.

"Hey," a voice called out.

I turned to see Todd Seaver.

"I heard the news," he said.

"About Kelly? Yeah, me too."

"Who cares about Kelly? Most likely she passed out because she's on one of those water and banana diets. I was talking about you. I heard you took first in the race on Saturday."

I stopped thinking about Joann and focused in on Todd. He shifted back and forth, like standing still was difficult for him. He cracked his knuckles and gave me a lazy smile.

"Where did you hear about my race?"

"I have spies," he said, and my eyes must have widened a bit because he started to laugh. "Promise me you haven't gone all conspiracy theory on me like the rest of this place."

"No, I just was surprised. No one follows track." I didn't mention that even my friends couldn't care less about my races. I looked away from his face. I hadn't noticed that he had dimples before, or maybe he'd never smiled at me before.

"Coach Attley was posting the times on the board up front and I saw it. Looks like you've got a shot at state finals again."

"I hope so. I'm up for a track scholarship." How did he know I went to state finals last year? I shot a look to the side to see if anyone was paying attention to us. For most of high school the male population never knew I was alive, and now I seemed to have two guys who were paying attention to me, both of them wildly inappropriate, since one was my best friend's guy and the other was the school pariah.

"You thinking of the Purdue regional campus in Fort Wayne?"

"Northwestern," I said, already raising my chin in defense of the usual spiel people gave me. *Why would you want to go there? It's so far away, and in the city. With crime. And brown people.*

"My older brother goes there."

"Really?" I had to fight the urge to grab his arm and cling to it. Here was proof positive that there were people who got out of Wheaton.

"Yeah, we lived in Chicago before here."

"Why did you move to Wheaton?"

"My family is in the witness protection program." He gave a laugh. "My dad's job means we get transferred."

"Still, what did you do wrong to end up at TES?"

"My parents liked the idea of 'small-town living.' My older brother went through this phase when he was in high school where he smoked a bit too much weed. 'Too much' being any weed, in my parents' opinion. They figured I couldn't get into any trouble if I went to school here."

We both snorted with the absurdity of that idea. Sometimes parents had no clue. He opened his mouth to say something else when there was a scream from the girls' bathroom. Everyone took a few steps back, and Mrs. Lamont, the home ec teacher, ran in. She popped out two seconds later.

"Call 911! We've got a girl down," she yelled, and a few girls in the hall screamed or started crying. They held on to one another, the boys standing in front of them as if we were standing on the deck of the *Titanic* and they were willing to sacrifice themselves.

Suddenly I saw Joann. She was standing near a bank of lockers. Her arms were crossed over her chest, and she looked as if she might cry. She looked at me as if to say, *I told you so* and then slipped away in the crowd.

"Christ, they're dropping like flies," said Todd. "Have you noticed it seems to be all the popular girls who're getting sick? It's become the new 'in' thing."

"Yeah, I noticed."

"Couldn't happen to a better group of girls, if you ask me. The only people I know whose conversational ability improves by being unconscious," Todd muttered.

Mr. Reilly appeared out of nowhere and yanked Todd by his sleeve.

"Watch your mouth," he grumbled, and then pointed us down the hall, where teachers were herding us all toward the cafeteria.

13

God, the traditional image of you with the long white beard and robes, a sort of Dumbledore type, makes you look serious. I have a feeling you've got a sense of humor. Granted, sometimes your humor seems a bit inappropriate, but it is funny. Especially when the joke isn't on me.

It was the TES version of the Black Plague. All we needed was someone to wander the halls yelling, "Bring out your dead."

Amy Winters was the girl who passed out in the bathroom. She would later get in trouble for packing lipstick. TES frowned on makeup, but it wasn't outlawed unless it was found to be "excessive." Several parents, however, were very anti-makeup. As far as Amy's parents were concerned, the tube of Berry Cherry she was caught with might as well have been a vial of crack cocaine. First a girl starts putting on lipstick, and the next thing you know it's crotchless panties and pole dancing. Lucky for her she was already in the hospital, otherwise her dad might have put her there.

After Amy went down at eight twenty a.m., word spread down the halls that Susan Abramo slumped over during freshman religion class around nine forty-five. In all fairness, it was probably a boring lecture. Mr. Reilly does the same talk every year for freshmen on why evolution is nothing more than a bunch of hooey. He's a strict Adam and Eve believer. There's a rumor that Mr. Reilly won't eat apples in case God still has something against the fruit. He gets really worked up about the idea that anyone would think he descended from a monkey. Susan fell into the aisle about three-quarters of the way through the lecture, when he was just gearing up for his big finish, where he hoots like an orangutan.

Carol Lang, Paula Swan, and Jennifer Furby all passed out in the cafeteria over lunch. At first there was some brief discussion that it might have been due to some type of sauerkraut foodborne illness, but no one really believed that was the case. As far as all of Wheaton was concerned, someone was targeting the popular girls.

When Tessa Townston collapsed in biology at approximately twelve forty-five p.m., dragging her Mendel's pea plant experiment to the floor with her, parents started to show up at the school to get their kids. At two o'clock the school sent us all home.

By six o'clock it made the local news in Fort Wayne.

"Do you have the TV on?" Colin asked as soon as I picked up the phone.

"I'm stretching. I'm going out for a run right now."

"Give it a break, Speed Racer, and turn on the TV. Wheaton's hit the big time."

"Wheaton?"

"Call me after." Colin clicked off, and I turned on the TV. The anchor, a woman in a blistering bright red dress and perfect hair, was seated at the news desk, a photo of TES behind her.

"Tonight, a story out of Wheaton. More than half a dozen young girls have been stricken with a mysterious illness over the past three days, with five girls falling ill today alone. Local hospital staff declined to comment, but the family physician of one girl indicated that there is suspicion of foul play.

"All the girls have regained consciousness and are undergoing further medical testing. The afflicted girls attend Trinity Evangelical Secondary School, which closed early today to allow the remainder of the student body to go home. School officials were unwilling to comment on whether the school will reopen tomorrow. Police stated that the investigation was ongoing, but it appears as if someone is deliberately making the girls sick." The anchorwoman shook her head slowly, as if she were reporting on a tragedy of tsunami-type proportions.

"You have to wonder if there's any place our kids are safe today," the male co-anchor chimed in. "When small-town America's in the crosshairs, then it's a sad day for every town." He shook his head in tandem with the woman anchor. They looked grim and serious. Suddenly her head popped up with a huge smile.

"Now a story from our series on Nutty Neighbors! We're profiling a fellow in the Franke Park area who is such a Wizards fan, he's painted his house in the baseball team's colors, complete with a giant mural of the mascot on the garage door!"

I clicked off the TV and grabbed the phone.

"I don't believe it," I said when Colin picked up.

"I know. Who would paint his house like that? The blue and green is one thing, but the silver trim?"

"Ha ha. Seriously, I can't believe it made the news. And what's with everyone getting sick all of a sudden? There's nothing wrong with anyone. Aren't there real events happening in the world that the news should be paying attention to? War? Environmental issues?"

"Some natural disaster somewhere?"

"Exactly." I pulled on my ponytail while I thought it over. "Maybe we should talk to someone. Tell them what we saw that night."

"What about Joann?"

"We could explain to her that nothing was going on, that I just had to get out of my house. I mean, it's the truth."

"And we just forgot to mention it until now?"

I stood and paced the living room. I had too much energy to sit still.

"There was nothing to mention. I mean, you guys seem to be doing better than ever."

"What does that mean?"

"It doesn't mean anything. Just that you guys seem like things are going well."

"What do you want from me? You were crystal clear, you're not interested."

I sighed. Is there anything worse than having someone throw your own words back at you? As a woman, I thought I was supposed to have the right to change my mind at will.

"She's mad at me," I said, changing the subject and feeling like I was breaking some kind of secret vow. I never talked to Colin about Joann. It felt like cheating on her. When your best friend dates your other best friend, you have to have some boundaries, things that you lock in a vault and don't discuss. My problem was that Colin was the only one I could think of to talk to who might know how to handle the current problem.

"I know, she told me."

Apparently Joann does not have the same feeling about the vault.

"She talks about me?"

"Not all the time."

"So why is she so pissed? Just because I want to move away?"

"She thinks you don't want to be her friend anymore."

"I don't? Then why is it that she's the one who won't talk to me?"

"Don't ask me."

"I would ask her, but she doesn't pick up the phone. Look, I want to move away, and I'm not going to apologize for that. This town isn't for me. I can't help it. I never meant to make her feel like I think she's a loser because she wants to stay in Wheaton."

"You didn't mean to make her feel like a loser, but you think she is."

"I do not!"

"Whatever."

"Now you're pissed?"

"I'm not pissed, but I'm not going to tell you something just to make you feel better. You do think people who want to stay in Wheaton are weird."

"You make it sound like this whole thing is my fault."

"Not everything is about someone being at fault."

"Thank you for that wisdom. Maybe you can become the first dairy-farming Buddha," I said. I could feel my breath coming more quickly, and I hadn't even started running yet.

Colin laughed.

"Dairy Buddha. I like that. Maybe I'll get real fat and get people to rub my belly for luck. Grow myself some udders." He let out a loud *mooooooo*.

"You're such an ass."

"I think that's why you love me."

"Now you've discovered my real feelings," I said with sarcasm. "I can't stay away from you."

"Like Todd?"

"What!" I felt my heart speed up, as if I'd been caught doing something wrong.

"A bunch of people saw you guys hanging out today."

you?"

ɪd at *me*?

ɦing with

red-hot.

at Joann

picked at

s incident

ed at me

'ever, but

ʒht when

year.

to sound

. What's

been the

ɫaration.

ok what

ead *The*

, a ten-minute conversation

ɦe quality. It sounded like you

ɦy." My face flushed.

ɪng to go out with someone,

l?"

im, he just doesn't seem like

ɪlin shrugging, which he does

ɪe indifferent.

ʏhat my type is?"

ɪnoying?"

et some ice cream?"

ɪroduct. I know I'm the dairy

ɪrter than the average person

ed with milk, but most people

: shouldn't tell anyone about

"I don't think it's a good idea."

"Because you don't want Joann to be mad a

"What makes you think she's going to be m You called me and asked me to go out."

"I did not ask you out. I asked you to do some me. There is a huge difference." I felt my face flus "You're making this sound like it's my fault."

"It's not about blame, I'm just pointing out is going to be mad at you."

I didn't say anything for a moment and instea the fringe on the pillow. After the great Christmas k there had been no doubt that Joann was more ti than at Colin. I guess the theory that friends are f boyfriends come and go, doesn't hold the same we the friend is planning to move away at the end of th

"She'd be mad at you, too," I said, trying no like I was sulking.

"I know. That's why I don't want you to te the point? Do you want us to break up?"

I swallowed the urge to point out that I hadn one to make the big "I've always loved you" de All I wanted was to get out of the house, and had happened. I should have stayed home and r *Princess Diaries*. Meg Cabot never let me down.

"Besides, it isn't just about me. Have you thought about track?" asked Colin.

"What about it?"

"You admit to being at a party with liquor, and you're off the track team. It's a violation of the TES moral code that you signed. Off the team, and there goes your scholarship."

I sat down with a whoosh. I felt like I had suddenly belly flopped into an ice-cold lake. I could picture the whole thing. TES has this form you have to sign where you pretty much vow to be absolutely perfect. You even have to promise to keep your thoughts pure. How they would know if you kept that one I have no idea, but I knew Colin was right. Even though we never went into the party, the fact that we were there and didn't turn anyone in would be enough to pull my track team eligibility. No track, no scholarship. No scholarship, no out-of-state tuition. No out-of-state tuition, and I would be staying in Wheaton.

Shit.

"I think I'm going to go for a run," I said finally. I clicked off the phone without waiting for him to say anything else. I sat on the sofa for a minute. I started chewing on my fingernails, something I hadn't done for years. It wasn't as if I wanted to be involved in the whole mess, but I felt like I had an out.

What the hell would Jesus do in this kind of situation? I paused to see if any heavenly advice was forthcoming. Nothing. Jesus had a knack for staying out of these kinds of situations.

I wasn't sure what Jesus would do, but I was going to run.

faked her church seizure (coincidence that she was dressed up on that Sunday? I don't think so) to take the pressure off Kimberly. I'm sure she convinced Kimberly that if she were sick too, no one would suspect what really happened. I'm betting Darci left out the part about how she couldn't stand Kimberly getting all the attention. Darci didn't play second to anyone, including, maybe in particular, her best friend. Why other people were passing out was a bit more confusing. I would assume Darci was poisoning her friends, except for the fact that Darci never did anything that would require her to share the limelight. My best guess is that just like Ugg boots, which became hugely popular despite the fact they made everyone look like cavewomen, passing out had become the cool thing. The way things stood now, if you didn't pass out, the assumption was that you must not be popular enough to be attacked. No wonder everyone was falling over.

The town appeared split on the issue of having the school reopen, based on an official poll taken by the cashier girls at the Stop & Shop. Half the town was of the mind that we should cancel school until we could assure the safety of everyone, and the other half didn't want to let the terrorists win. I was keeping my fingers crossed that school would be open; otherwise I would be stuck at home all day doing something mind-numbing like pulling everything off the shelves and dusting. For the first time in my life, when the alarm went off at six thirty, instead of rolling over, stuffing the pillow over my head, and cursing the existence of TES, I leaped out of bed and scurried to get ready. I was actually at school early. As I walked through the halls I tried not to notice that Todd was right, everyone did dress like an ad from Eddie Bauer.

"Emma!"

I looked down the hall to see who was calling my name and saw Joann weaving through the crowds. She was waving. She was also wearing khakis with her uniform sweater, not that I was noticing.

"Hey," she said when she was close. "How's your ankle?"

"Okay. It was a little stiff this morning, but otherwise it's fine."

"I was going to call you," Joann mumbled, looking at her feet.

"Yeah, I was going to call you, too," I said.

"Look, about Darci being over at my place," she started.

"Hey, you can have anyone over you want."

"I know that. I just meant I didn't want you to be pissed. Darci can be okay."

I raised an eyebrow.

"No, seriously, she comes across a bit high-and-mighty sometimes, but she's okay. Besides, I thought it would be good to be involved with stuff. What with everyone being sick, I wanted to offer to help with the dance."

"Fair enough."

We stood looking at each other for a few beats.

"How weird was it that Todd showed up?"

"He ended up giving me a ride," I said.

"Are you serious?"

"Yeah." I didn't say anything about going out to the drive-in. It wasn't that it was a secret, or that I thought she would make fun of me, but it felt private and I wasn't ready to share.

"Get out." She gave me a shove. "How is it we don't talk for a day and I missed so much?"

"I'm a very happening person. You have to stick close."

"Or risk being left behind?"

I took her by the elbow, and we started walking toward homeroom. I kept looking around as we walked, but there was no sign of Todd. It wasn't that I thought he was going to show up at my locker with a dozen roses, but I thought it was odd I hadn't seen him at all.

"Left behind? Does Batman leave Robin behind?

Would you have Mickey without Minnie? Jennifer Aniston without Courteney Cox? Chocolate without vanilla?"

"Anyone ever tell you that you're seriously odd?"

"All the time, but you're my best friend, so what does it say about you?"

17

God, the whole boy-girl thing is fairly complicated. No wonder you left coming up with Adam and Eve until the very end of your creation project. I mean, look at Adam and Eve. They had relationship issues and they were the only ones in the garden. Eve had one guy to worry about and one apple to avoid. No wonder it's so complicated with me. I've got too many choices and way too many temptations.

Mr. Pointer teaches all the math courses at TES. He is not a happy man. The close proximity to numbers all these years must have done something to him. Mr. Pointer looks like a character out of one of the Lord of the Rings movies, and I don't mean one of the handsome elf types, either. He's tall and freakishly skinny, with a thin hooked nose that makes him look a bit like a bird. Rumors have existed forever that Mr. Pointer is gay. He's not married and shows no inclination to give it a try, which around here is pretty much enough to label him as light in the loafers. Then you add the fact that he spends a lot of time on his hair, buffs his nails, and wears fancy silk argyle socks, and he might as well take out a full-page ad in *Out* magazine. Of course, if he is gay, he's got the entire faculty of TES and the community saying on a daily basis that he's damned to eternal hell, which is enough to make anyone a bit irritable, so the whole mood issue could be related to that instead of math.

I've never gotten the anti-gay thing. If you could choose your sexuality and choose to be gay or straight, then I imagine there would be lobby groups trying to get you to change your mind. It would be like long-distance companies. They would have telemarketers that would call you at home and try and convince you to change sides, maybe throw in three free months of high-speed Internet service or a toaster. If it isn't a choice, then it means you must be born a certain way, either gay or straight. If you are born that way, it must mean that God made you that way, which makes it seem unlikely that he would damn you to hell for it. After all, it would be technically his fault.

Regardless of why Mr. Pointer is in a chronically bad mood, it is clear the only thing that gives him any joy is making his students' lives miserable. We are required to sit according to how we did on the last test. The worst student is in the front row, right-hand side, and the next worst next to them, and so on, with the best student being in the back row. If that weren't enough, his favorite way to teach is to call you to the board and have you write down how you did a particular problem. Then you have to stand there next to your work while your fellow classmates (traitors) point out what you did wrong. If I manage to get out of TES without requiring some serious therapy, it's going to be a miracle.

Joann passed me a note.

DO YOU LIKE TODD?

I chewed on the end of my pencil while I thought it over. I didn't see any point in telling her that just a short time ago I was trying to figure out if I liked her boyfriend. I also didn't see any point in sending back a note asking if she was really sure she liked Colin or not. I looked down at her note and thought about Todd. He was interesting, but is interest the same as liking someone? Maybe it was a chemical thing. Maybe Todd made more pheromones than the average guy. I shifted in my seat as I remembered how I felt when his finger had outlined my lips. I pushed a shred of eraser out of my mouth.

No.

Joann read the note and looked over at me, one eyebrow raised in disbelief. I had a feeling I was busted.

No? R U SURE?

Okay, not sure. What do you think: interesting or odd?

I lobbed the note back to Joann when Mr. Pointer was at the board detailing a complex problem where two trains left two stations at different times. This is what educators spend their energy on? I'm not planning to go into transportation logistics. I can see no value in learning how to work out this kind of problem. If you didn't know when the train was going to show up, why wouldn't you simply ask at the information desk or go online and print out a train schedule?

Joann placed the note under her shoe and then slid it across the aisle to me. I placed my foot on it and slid it under my desk. I waited until Mr. Pointer was busy and then bent over to pick it up. I was unfolding it under the desk when Mr. Pointer called my name. I yanked my head up, certain we had been caught. I briefly considered shoving the note into my mouth to destroy the evidence. There was no way I would allow this to be read aloud. I had enough problems without people pointing out that I was dating the school leper. I would rather die choking on ruled paper.

"I said, you are needed in the office, Ms. Proctor,"

Mr. Pointer said, his voice showing the annoyance he felt at having to repeat himself.

I heard a few people whispering, and when I turned to the door, my eyes widened. Kimberly's dad, the chief of police, was outside the door wearing his full cop getup and standing next to Mr. Karp, our principal. I pointed to myself and Mr. Karp nodded. I may be only seventeen, but I'm smart enough to know that when the cops come to pick you up it's pretty much guaranteed to be bad news.

I stood up slowly. I shoved the note from Joann into my pocket unread.

"You should bring your things. You most likely won't be returning to class," Mr. Karp said. My classmates were really whispering now, and Joann raised an eyebrow at me. I gave her a small shrug, picked up my books, and followed Mr. Karp out into the hall.

18

God, I soooooooo don't need to be in any more trouble than I already am. If you could see it in your heart to get me out of this particular situation, I am completely willing to make it up to you. If you get me out of this, I hereby vow all of the following:

- *I will never again let Paula at the Dairy Hut give me a large cone for a small cone price when her boss isn't there. I also will forgo free sprinkles, chocolate dipping, and extra spoonfuls of those crushed Heath bars.*
- *I will not make fun of Darci, even when she richly deserves it.*
- *When my mom asks me to clean my room, I will not simply stuff things under the bed.*
- *While attending church services, I will pay attention to Reverend Evers and not engage*

in unholy fantasies revolving around Johnny Depp dragging me off to be his pirate queen.

Despite my poor attitude, I am generally not someone who spends a lot of time in the principal's office. Mr. Karp and Officer Ryan didn't say a word as they walked down the hall, with me trailing after them. I had the feeling that we were going to get to Mr. Karp's office and there would be an electric chair in there. Considering how much TES preached the value of life, they were huge fans of the death penalty. I wondered if they were going to torture a confession out of me, Guantanamo style. I wondered if they would tell me what I was accused of or stick with the silent treatment. The problem with the silent treatment is that you can end up confessing to something that they didn't even know about. I could think of nothing I had done that merited police action, but it was possible I was in trouble for any of the following:

- Two weeks ago I had left a bunch of PETA "Fur Is Murder" flyers in the library return box. Mrs. Tucker, our librarian, always wears this nasty fox fur coat. It looks like it was dead and buried and then she dug it up to make a coat out of it.

- I smuggled my iPod into last Friday's school church service (because going on Sunday apparently isn't enough for the under-eighteen set). We were supposed to be meditating on how we could make the world a better place by sharing the Word of the Lord, and instead I had been rocking out to Fergie.
- We were supposed to go door-to-door and pass out leaflets on the church's missionary appeal. The idea was that our youthful enthusiasm would make others want to hand us gobs of money that would be used to purchase Bibles for the missionaries to distribute. Personally, based on pictures I'd seen, I felt Third World countries needed fresh water and fly repellent more than Bibles. At any rate, instead of passing mine out, I'd stuffed them in a shoebox under my bed.
- TES has this theory that evil thoughts are as bad as evil deeds. If anyone knew half the things I'd been thinking about lately, I could be in big trouble.

Mr. Karp's office was grim. No wonder he spent so much time wandering the hallways. It was clear that Mr. Karp did not watch the Home & Garden network. His desk was flat gray metal and his chair let out squeals and groans of protest every time he moved. The walls were a dingy white-gray color, and he had a giant framed picture of the Crucifixion on the back wall. On the other wall he had pictures of himself taken with what passed for important people in Wheaton, like the mayor and the owner of the Stop & Shop. The top of the desk was neat, with tidy piles of paper and folders stacked to the side. I sat in a hard wooden chair directly across from him. Officer Ryan sat off to the side. I gave him a tentative smile, but he didn't smile back.

"Do you know why you're here, Emma?" Mr. Karp asked.

I shook my head.

"Is there anything you want to tell me about what's been happening lately?" he said meaningfully.

I took a deep breath. Colin must have confessed about us being at the Barn.

Shit.

Was this it? Was I about to lose my track eligibility? And why was Officer Ryan here? Was I going to

be arrested for hiding underage drinking? TES has a real thing for reformed sinners. I could work up some big tears if it would help. In fact, it might not be that hard to work them up. My lower lip was already starting to shake. My stomach was in free fall. My throat felt too tight to let the words out.

"You need to tell us what you know about Todd," Mr. Karp said.

My brain screeched to a halt.

"Todd?"

"We know the two of you are friends."

"Todd Seaver?" I asked, in case there was a mystery Todd somewhere.

"Playing stupid isn't going to help," Officer Ryan said, his voice stern.

Mr. Karp looked over at him and then back to me.

"You don't need to be frightened, Emma. Officer Ryan isn't here in an official capacity. He's the head of the parent advisory board and is helping us sort this situation out."

Officer Ryan didn't look like he was here in an unofficial capacity. He had on his uniform, complete with his Batman belt of police accessories. His hand rested on his Taser as if he was hoping I would make a break for the

door. I wondered what he would do if I told him that the problem wasn't Todd; it was his pharmaceutical-swilling daughter Kimberly.

"Mr. Reilly told us he overheard Todd Seaver telling you that it 'couldn't happen to a better group of girls.' Is that correct?" asked Officer Ryan.

"It was just a joke."

"You think it's funny to joke about people getting hurt? That strikes your funny bone?"

"Now, now, let's not get ahead of ourselves," Mr. Karp said.

I turned to face him.

"Now you admit Todd said that?" Mr. Karp said, leaning forward.

"Well, yes, but he didn't mean anything by it," I said.

"Todd hasn't made a lot of friends here at Trinity. How well do you know him, Emma?"

"We've only talked a couple of times. He seems like a nice guy," I offered.

"Only a couple of times? We have someone who saw you get into a car with him yesterday."

God, I hate this town. It's like being on a reality TV show where there's a camera on in every room. Big Brother . . . Wheaton-style.

"I fell yesterday when I was running, and he took me home." I held out my elbow, pulling up the sleeve so the road rash could be seen.

"And he took you straight home?" Officer Ryan asked, stressing the word "straight." The question smacked of one they already knew the answer to.

"No." I drew the word out. "We went out to the Night Light and talked for a bit." There was a long silence. "We were looking at the stars."

"Looking at stars? So that's what they call it these days." Officer Ryan chuckled. Mr. Karp gave him a grim look and he stopped short, like a boy caught telling jokes during church service.

"What can you tell us about Todd, Emma?"

"Well, he's from the Chicago area, but I'm guessing you know that from his school records. He likes horses and science. He's into astronomy." I shot Officer Ryan a look. "Not astrology. It's different, you know."

"That's not what we're interested in. How does he feel about the kids here at Trinity? Did he ever make any comments about hating it here?"

"I'm not sure people here are that nice to him."

"What do you mean?"

"It's not a great place if you're not from here. I don't

think he ever really fit in very well, and this is the kind of place where fitting in is really important."

"There you go. Fits the profile," Officer Ryan said, slapping his hand down on his thigh.

"Profile?" I asked. I had the feeling that the reason that Officer Ryan was involved was one part because it involved his daughter, one part because he loved to stick his nose in things, and one big healthy dose of him watching too many episodes of *CSI*.

"There is an allegation that Mr. Seaver has been mixed up in the recent events here. We looked through his locker and found some suspicious items."

"You think Todd Seaver is poisoning TES?" I asked in disbelief. "You think he's trying to take down the school one popular girl at a time?"

"You said yourself that he hates his fellow students and doesn't fit in. He's quiet, most likely has some repressed rage over how he feels he's been treated."

"That's not what I said." I paused. "You're twisting my words all around."

"Did he confess to you how he was poisoning the girls?"

"What? No."

"Emma, it's important that you're honest with us." Mr. Karp leaned forward on his elbows. "You don't need to worry.

I understand. The devil is attractive. This is how he pulls us in. I can imagine you must have been flattered to have a boy paying attention to you. Maybe he used flattery. It can be easy to have our heads turned. We should pray about it." Mr. Karp took my hands in his, but I yanked mine back.

"You think Todd is the devil?" I decided not to address the issue of him basically making it sound as if I were some kind of loser who would follow anyone who paid attention to me. Suddenly everyone seemed to feel it was important to point out just how unpopular I really was.

"I think the devil was in him. Must have been, to make him do something like this." Mr. Karp shook his head and turned to Officer Ryan. "She's right, you know. The boy never did fit in well here. He doesn't participate in many of the school activities."

"He's Jewish. Wouldn't it be a bit funny for him join the Spirit Squad! or plan the Easter celebrations?" I asked.

"I hear they have that Jews for Jesus thing," Officer Ryan offered up.

I wanted to run screaming from the room. It was like being trapped in some kind of weird alternate reality. Somehow I was now responsible for defending Todd (the lip toucher), when I wasn't even sure how I felt about him.

"Look, I really don't think Todd had anything to do with the situation. I mean, it's possible that the girls are doing it to themselves, you know how people hate to be left out of stuff."

Officer Ryan crossed his arms over his chest. I got the feeling he wasn't buying it.

"Plus, it's not just Todd. There are a lot of people who don't like some of the popular kids, but it doesn't mean they would do anything to them."

"Who else?" Mr. Karp pulled a pad of paper over to get down the names. "It's possible he didn't act alone. It could be like that trench coat mafia."

"Trench coat mafia?" Were they kidding me? This was Wheaton, maybe a denim overall mafia or the polo shirt mafia, but *trench coat*?

"Is it your statement, Ms. Proctor, that you had no awareness that Mr. Seaver was involved in the recent events?"

"No. I mean yes. I mean I don't think he did anything."

"As the investigation continues, it would look very bad if we were to discover you've been suppressing evidence related to this case," Officer Ryan said, looking at me meaningfully as if he meant to bring down the entire power of the parent advisory board onto my head. I slunk down slightly.

I'm pretty sure not mentioning what Colin and I saw that night at the Barn might technically fall into the category of evidence suppression.

"I think we should take just a moment to pray for a successful outcome for this investigation, and to thank the Lord for keeping our children safe," Mr. Karp said. They both bent their heads. There was a long pause while apparently each of them communicated with our Lord. What would Jesus do if he were on *Law & Order*?

"What kind of proof do you have against Todd?" I blurted out.

"Emma!" Mr. Karp barked. "What's gotten into you?" I couldn't tell if he was angry that I had interrupted him at prayer or that I was questioning him. I'm guessing he liked me better as a pod person.

"What makes you so sure he did anything?" I tried again, avoiding Mr. Karp's eyes.

"We can't give you all the details, of course, but as you probably know, some strange drugs were found in Kimberly's system. Mr. Seaver spent a significant amount of his free time in the chemistry lab, where he would have access to those substances," Officer Ryan said.

"But there are tons of kids who take chem."

"You need to look at the whole picture. Mr. Seaver

also had the means of distribution. He had detention that required him to work through some lunch periods in the cafeteria. We believe he slipped the drugs into the girls' food."

"Those girls don't eat, they just push their food around. No one here eats the hot lunch, and tons of kids work in the cafeteria. Besides, I heard no one other than Kimberly tested positive for drugs."

"Looks like this young lady is studying to be a defense lawyer." Officer Ryan chuckled as if being condescending was the height of humor.

"Where's Todd?" I asked.

"Mr. Seaver is at home with his parents."

"I really don't think Todd had anything to do with this," I tried again. I was trying to formulate a way to explain how I knew this without calling Kimberly a lying lush to her gun-toting dad's face, having it come out that I had been out with Colin, losing my best friend, and getting kicked off the track team, all at the same time, when there was a knock at the door.

Mrs. Sealy, the receptionist, leaned in, looking flustered. She handed Mr. Karp a note. He read it quickly and stood up. It looked like our meeting was over.

"Another girl has passed out," Mr. Karp said, passing the note to Officer Ryan.

I fought the urge to roll my eyes. You would think TES would have run out of popular girls seeking attention.

"Emma, perhaps you should stop by the first aid room and talk with this young woman. It might change your mind about keeping any secrets."

The last thing I wanted to do was sit vigil next to a hysterical popular wannabe with Darci and her cronies.

"I should really get back to math," I said, trying to put a hint of regret into my voice, as if the allure of my education was just too much. Officer Ryan had a strange smile on his face, and a minute before the words left his mouth I had a horrible feeling what he was going to say.

"Are you sure? It's Joann."

19

God, does math come easily to you? I notice you didn't seem to have any trouble with multiplying loaves and fishes. Maybe that should be our story problem. "If you are the Son of God and have to feed a crowd of several hundred, how many times will you have to increase the loaves and fishes to meet the needs of the crowd, assuming each crowd member wants one fish and one loaf? Then rework the problem assuming 25 percent of the crowd are vegetarians and won't eat the fish, but will want double the bread."

Joann lay on the cot in the first aid room. Calling it a first aid room is really a bit of a stretch. TES is too small of a school to afford a trained health professional and a separate space for first aid needs. In reality, the first aid room is a large supply closet with a cot and a gym teacher who wishes he had gone to medical school. That gym teacher, Mr. Hansen, was holding Joann's limp wrist, taking her pulse. His face was grim and serious, as if at any moment he would have to perform open-heart surgery on her using only a Bic pen and his shoelaces. Mr. Pointer stood to the side with his arms crossed, no doubt devastated to have his train speed lecture interrupted. Joann's eyes widened when she saw me at the door. I raised a hand in greeting.

"Ms. Proctor?" said Mr. Pointer, looking at me. "If your meeting with Mr. Karp is over, you need to report back to class, that is, unless you got lost."

"I needed to stop in here before coming back," I said. "I have a, uh, women's issue." My face flushed, but it was nothing compared to Mr. Pointer's reaction. He took a step back, as if I had admitted to having a small problem with the Ebola virus. He gave a brisk nod and without another word left the room, leaving my female issues up to more trained professionals. Clearly he was afraid of some kind of wild menstruation breakout. Mr. Hansen gave me an annoyed look. He had a real medical emergency on his hands; he didn't want to have to deal with something as common as a period.

"I'll get the key to the feminine product machine in the ladies' room. Will you wait here with Joann in case she starts to feel lightheaded again?"

Both of us looked down at Joann. She was doing her best to look wan and frail, like a Victorian lady with the vapors.

"I'll just lie here till my mom comes," Joann said in a soft, whispery voice.

Mr. Hansen patted her shoulder, as if she was being very brave and she might not make it until he returned. I was getting nauseated with all this drama. Once Mr. Hansen left I sat down on the end of the cot. Joann propped herself up on her elbows.

"You're getting your period?" She rummaged through her purse, looking for her emergency stash of supplies. Joann had a black hole of a purse that contained everything you might need for up to a two-week camping trip.

"No, I heard what happened and wanted to see you." Joann's eyes shifted away from me.

"What did Officer Ryan want?" she asked.

"They think Todd is behind all the stuff that's been happening. They're implying that he was planning some kind of school violence, a terrorist attack thing."

Joann's eyes went wide. Suddenly she didn't look so ill; she looked excited to be on the ground floor of what was sure to be prime TES gossip.

"Wow," she said finally. "I can't believe he did that. I

mean, I knew he was different, but still." Her voice trailed off as she shook her head. I looked at her with my mouth falling open.

"What are you talking about? Todd didn't do anything."

"You just told me the police said he's behind everything."

"I said the police *think* he's behind everything. There's a difference."

"You know, Todd never liked Darci and Kimberly."

"No one likes them."

"Well, someone likes them or they wouldn't be popular. Everyone makes judgments about them, and they're really nice."

I had to fight the urge to roll my eyes. It wasn't that long ago that Joann couldn't stand Darci or Kimberly, but I guess all had been forgiven now that they had joined forces on important issues like making sure the spring dance was a success.

"They're saying he slipped something into the food when he was working in the caf."

"I always thought it was a bad idea to make us work off detentions in the cafeteria. I heard Kyle spit into the mac and cheese when he was there."

"Maybe Kyle did it."

"Do you think he was involved?" Joann lowered her voice.

"No, I don't, but what do you think? Did anything taste funny in your lunch today?" I smacked my forehead as if just realizing something. "I totally forgot. You brought your lunch, didn't you? Puts a hole in the whole hot lunch distribution theory."

"Yeah, I guess." Joann didn't meet my eyes.

"The important thing is, Todd didn't do anything to anyone."

"How do you know? I mean, is it possible that your crush on him is blurring the facts for you?"

"I don't have a crush," I said.

Joann gave me a knowing smile with a raised eyebrow.

"What? I don't have a thing for him. Maybe—and I mean this is at best—maybe I am mildly intrigued with the guy. He's a bit different. He's nice. I wouldn't mind getting to know him better. It is a million miles away from being in love and wanting to date him."

"I didn't say love, I said like."

"Are you listening to me? I don't like him. Only in this town does talking to a guy once or twice mean that you want to have his future children."

"Fine," Joann said, giving a tired sigh.

"So what happened?"

Joann's face flushed red, and she looked away again.

"I suddenly felt really lightheaded and the light seemed all funny, and the next thing I knew I must have passed out, because I woke up with Mr. Pointer looking down at me."

"Well that should give you nightmares for a few years."

Joann gave a nervous laugh.

"You've never passed out before," I said, pointing out the obvious. "Did you skip breakfast or something?"

"I didn't fake it, if that's what you think."

"I didn't say you did."

"I'm not saying anyone did anything to me. Maybe I just passed out."

"There's a lot of that going around these days."

Joann opened her mouth but didn't have a chance to speak before Darci swooped in like the angel of death.

"Oh. My. God! Kimberly just told me what happened." Darci held her hands up near her heart, as if she had just received the news that Joann had been mauled to death in a tragic tractor accident. "I told Justin to find Colin and tell him what happened. I'm sure he'll want to be here."

"I'm fine too, in case you were concerned," I said.

Darci looked over at me and then chose to ignore me. She sat on the edge of the cot and rubbed Joann's arm.

"Someone's got to do something." Darci shook her head in disgust. "What is the school waiting for, someone to be killed? Didn't I tell you just the other day that you were at risk?"

"I gotta go," I said. Both of them looked at me. Joann seemed surprised that I was still there.

"Take care of yourself," said Joann. I'm sure she didn't mean it the way it sounded, but it felt like a threat. I slipped out into the hallway. There was still no sign of Mr. Hansen. I couldn't fathom going back to math, and I didn't want to stay there and wait for Colin to rush to Joann's side. I felt the note Joann had passed me in math wadded up in my pocket. I pulled it out to see how she had responded to the Todd interesting or odd question. Her answer was at the bottom in her typical rounded printing that looked like cartoon lettering:

Interesting <u>and</u> odd.

I read it again. Interesting and odd. Just like my life.

I waited for a beat and then pushed open the door and walked out of the school.

20

God, I totally get why people in the Bible wandered out in the desert for forty days and forty nights—they wanted some time to themselves. One of the many problems with Indiana is there are no deserts. If you want some time to yourself around here, people won't leave you alone. They just keep asking, "What's wrong?" over and over until you feel like running away screaming. Maybe that's why Moses wandered off—he wanted to get out of his small town.

How boring is it if I admit I had never skipped school before? How did I make it to senior year without skipping a few classes? If I'm going to be this well behaved at seventeen, how boring am I going to be at thirty? There have been a few times when I stayed home "sick" when the only thing that was really wrong with me was being sick of school, but this was the first time I just flat-out skipped.

I froze outside the school door. I wondered if some kind of alarm would go off, as if I'd made a prison break. For all I knew a searchlight would pop out of the top of the building and a pack of wild German shepherds would be released to chase me down.

Nothing happened. I took slow deep breaths, waiting. Still nothing. I heard the bell go off inside and the sound of people moving around in the halls. There was the clang of lockers and the buzz of everyone talking. I gave the TES gossip network five minutes before everyone knew that Joann had joined the selected afflicted, and that Todd was suspended pending his status as chief suspect.

In fairy tales the beautiful princess is woken up with a kiss. For me everything went to hell with one kiss. Just one lousy kiss (that for the record, I really don't think should count, since I didn't know it was coming and it was over before I knew it started). Colin has been a part of my life for as long as I can remember, and I think I love the idea of him always being a part of my life more than I love him. With that kiss everything between us changed, and it spilled over to Joann and from her to the rest of the school. I gave the door one more look and then walked away.

I wanted to see Todd. When I told Joann I didn't like him, that might have been going a bit too far. I'm not saying that

I did like him, but rather that the situation was still unclear. I decided to wander casually past Todd's house. I wanted him to know that I had told the police I knew he didn't do it. When I rounded the corner to his street, I stopped in my tracks. The stay-at-home-mom brigade was outside his house. They had their strollers parked, their arms crossed, and their tongues wagging. It was the Wheaton version of villagers with torches and pitchforks. It hadn't taken long for the news to spread about the idea of Todd being mixed up in what was happening. It could turn ugly if Todd were to wander outside. If I walked up to the front door, I estimated it would take no less than five minutes for the word to spread that I was a member of Todd's poison gang. There was no way I could even walk past. They would be on their phones before I got ten paces. I turned and cut through the lawn and walked along the greenbelt that ran behind the street. I counted the houses to figure out which one was Todd's. I sat on the pine needles, trying to figure out what to do next. I waited, hoping Todd would walk past a window, but no such luck. His house appeared to be in lockdown mode. Then again, if I were being accused of taking out my classmates in an efficient poison plan I might lie low too. I waited another ten minutes and then walked up to the back of the house. I tried to look casual, like I might have just wandered into their backyard by accident. I didn't see anyone; they seemed to be all out front. I gave the back door a sharp knock. It seemed as loud as a cannon shot.

No one answered, and I was raising my hand to knock again when the door flew open.

"I told you to get away," Todd yelled in my face.

I wasn't sure what Todd was going to say when we saw each other again, but I hadn't expected that. I stood there with my arm still in knocking position and my mouth open.

"Emma?" Todd gave a quick look around and then pulled me into the house by my elbow. "I didn't know it was you. The holier-than-thou brigade has been stopping by all afternoon to let me know I'm damned to hell. I thought you were one of them." He looked over at the clock that hung in the kitchen. "What are you doing here? Shouldn't you be in class?"

"You know me, rebel with a cause."

"You cut class?" Todd looked impressed, as if I had displayed the ability to pull off a particularly tricky yoga maneuver.

"Karp called me into his office and asked me about you. He had Officer Ryan with him."

"They gave my parents a big song and dance about how the whole thing would be kept confidential while they did their investigation." Todd made finger quotations around the word "investigation."

"Shoot first, ask questions later, always a great TES motto. Just like Jesus would do."

"Don't forget, if it's different it's probably wrong."

"Or the time-honored favorite, guilty until we decide otherwise."

Todd gave a laugh. He looked at me.

"I didn't do this," he said, his voice suddenly serious.

"I know."

Todd smiled at me. He had this way of letting his smile creep up on his face, like slow-moving maple syrup. It started at one corner and then just slunk over to the other side.

"Things still complicated?"

"Less complicated."

Todd took a step closer so that we were inches apart. I could feel his breath on my face. Peppermint. I closed my eyes, leaning forward, waiting.

Nothing.

I opened one eye, peeking at him. He was smiling.

"I never do what's expected," he said.

"Me neither." Then before I could second-guess myself, I leaned in and kissed him. I could feel him start with surprise, but a second later he was kissing me back. He pulled

"Hey, you're home," I said, stating the obvious. She said nothing. Just sat there, staring. No doubt thinking of new and hideous punishments to mete out. I stood there, chewing on my lower lip. This was not going to go well. I gave my mouth a swipe, trying to tell if my lip gloss was smeared up the side of my face like a giant billboard screaming, "I've been skipping school and making out!" She kept looking at me as if she was waiting for something. "How was your day?"

"How do you think it was?" She said each word clipped and hard. It struck me as one of those questions that doesn't require a response. "The police came to my office today. Then they told me they had some questions for you and that you had snuck out of school. How do you think I felt with the police at my workplace asking about your involvement in these poisonings? Did you think how that would look to the people I work with? How do you think I felt hearing that you've been sneaking off to the drive-in theater with some boy?"

"I didn't sneak off."

She stood up quickly, and I backed up a step.

"Do not play your games with me today, Emma Elizabeth Proctor. This is not a debate."

"Sorry."

My mom gave a sigh and then walked into the kitchen

me tight to him, his hands caught up in my hair.

This was the kind of kiss that would wake up a princess. Heck, this was the kind of kiss that would wake the nearly dead. I could feel every atom of my skin; every nerve was standing on end, humming with energy.

Todd leaned back, taking a breath. We looked at each other, nearly panting.

"Well, that was unexpected," he said.

I shrugged. "I like the idea of keeping you on your toes."

"I have to say this was a pretty lousy day, but it's getting better."

"I would hate for you to have a bad day." And then we were kissing again. The phone rang, and we broke apart as if caught. Todd looked over.

"I should get that. My parents went to talk to a lawyer. Wait right here."

Todd reached for the phone. A lawyer. Suddenly the situation came rushing back to me. Todd was being accused and all I had to do was say what really happened and everything would go away. What would he say if he found out I knew all along? What would Joann say if I confessed I'd been at the Barn with Colin? Suddenly the room felt too small. I swallowed, my throat feeling tight. I reached up and touched my mouth. Todd was mumbling on the phone. He had a smear of my lip gloss on the side of his mouth.

I took a quick step back. Todd looked over, surprised.

I shook my head no. Todd cocked an eyebrow and held up a finger, wanting me to wait. I knew if he talked to me I was going to have to tell him everything, and I couldn't.

"Sorry," I whispered, and bolted out the back door.

2

It seems like as soon as I think things couldn't get any wors
you take that as a challenge. For the record, could you just t
leaving me alone? I seem to be perfectly capable of screwing
my own life without you making things worse. Before you s
anything—please don't point out that the majority of pro
lems are of my own making—that doesn't help. You're Go
after all—you parted the Red Sea. I have to think that if y
wanted to be more helpful to me, you could.

The instant I walked in the door to my house, it v
clear that instead of going over to Todd's, I should h
gone into some kind of witness protection program.
mom was sitting at the kitchen table. Not eating or dri
ing. Not reading or watching TV. Just sitting there, wai
for me to get home. It looked like her blood pressure
gone up a few valuable points.

and turned on the water in the sink full blast. She stood facing the wall without saying a word. It wasn't clear if the discussion was over and I was free to go or not.

"I do the best I can, Emma," she said softly.

"Mom, nothing happened. I fell while I was running, and Todd gave me a ride home. We sat and talked for a bit." I decided not to mention this afternoon. No need to muddy the water. "And it's not the police, it's Kimberly's dad. Officer Ryan is on the parent advisory board. You make it sound like the FBI is involved."

"You don't think it's bad enough as it is? Kimberly's parents are concerned. I'm concerned."

"There's nothing to be concerned about."

"Did he talk about what he's done?"

"He hasn't done anything."

She spun around.

"Oh, you know that for sure?" She sat down and motioned for me to sit at the table. "Look, you've lived here almost your whole life. You believe what people tell you, because people here are honest. I was the same way when I was your age. I thought I had the world all figured out. I was going to move out of here, shake the dust off my feet, and have some kind of grand adventure. Then I moved away and discovered that not every new experience is an adventure. Do you know how scared I was when I heard you've been hanging around with this boy? He could have hurt you."

"You believe Todd is some kind of lying, murdering rapist because he's not from around here? Of course instead of picking some usual way of acting out he's going to take out the popular girls one at a time using the dreaded home chemistry set. You're like everyone else. Just because he's different, he must be the one. If I'm not part of the pod, then you're not happy."

"No, Emma, I'm not judging Todd, but he's clearly got some issues that he has to get sorted out."

"What issues? You don't even know him!"

"Things were found in his possession, Emma." She paused. "Dangerous things."

"Like what?"

"He had several violent video games."

"Mom, they sell that stuff at Wal-Mart. Video games are not the great evil. They aren't even illegal."

"I know you want to protect this boy. Maybe you like him. Maybe you feel like he's the only one who understands you, and because he told you he had nothing to do with all of this, you want to believe it. I don't know if he drugged those girls or not. That's for the school to investigate, but until they do, you aren't going to see him or talk to him. Is that clear?"

"Are you kidding me? I'm graduating in a few months and you're going to tell me who I can hang out with and who I can't? I don't believe Todd's innocent just because he told me he didn't have anything to do with it. In fact, we've never even talked about it at all."

I swallowed. My throat felt tight and closed. This was it; it was time to come clean. I looked down at the table.

"Kimberly wasn't poisoned. She took the drugs herself."

"What?"

"I saw her. She was at a party, and she took a bunch of stuff. She was throwing up outside. She and Darci came up with the story about her being poisoned to cover up for the fact that they snuck out to go to the Barn. As far as everyone else, I don't know what's going on with them, but I think they're just flipping out." I said everything in a rush, the words spilling out faster and faster. It actually felt good to confess. My mom was quiet; she just looked at me for a long time.

"And you're saying this all happened last Friday," she said.

I nodded.

"Don't lie to me."

"I'm not lying."

"You were home that night, Emma. It was the night we had a fight and you ran off to your room."

"I snuck out."

"Emma, stop it. I looked in on you before I went to my room. You were asleep in your bed. I don't know if you think this story is helping Todd, but the whole thing is only going to make the situation worse."

I stood there with my mouth wide open. She didn't believe me. I was telling the truth and she didn't believe a word of it.

"I'm not lying. I'm telling the truth."

"Okay, that's it." My mom stood up, wiping her hands on her pants. "I talked to Reverend Evers today about all of this, and I think he's right."

"You talked to Reverend Evers about me?"

"I don't know what to make of you lately. I've done the best I can. It isn't easy to raise a child on your own. I brought you back here to grow up where you would have a family, so that all of Wheaton could be your family. I thought I knew what to do, but I'll admit I don't know what to do with you now."

"Why do you have to *do* anything with me?"

"This discussion is at an end. You're going to be spending the afternoons with Reverend Evers. He's got some things you can do at the church to help him. You're going to do that until this has sorted itself out. You need to get your focus back onto what's important."

"I can't go to the church in the afternoons. I've got track."

"No, you don't."

Everything in the room froze. There wasn't a sound. My lungs felt trapped, pinned down; I couldn't pull in a breath.

Mom stood up and moved back to the counter. She started wiping down the counters, as if Lysol could clean up all of our problems. "I called Coach Attley. You're off the team for right now. We'll re-evaluate the situation in another week or so," she said quietly.

"You can't pull me off the team." I looked around the room, as if a lifeboat would suddenly appear and pull me to safety. "The scholarship committee will be looking at my times. Missing any meets could blow my chances at getting a full ride." I grabbed her hand and held on to it. I was crying. "Mom, you know how important this is to me. You can't do this."

"The easy thing isn't the same as the right thing."

"You have to be joking. You can't!" My mind raced

in circles. Track was the only thing going well this year. If Northwestern didn't see good times, they might give their scholarship dollars to someone else. Shit. Shit. Shit.

"This isn't up for discussion. I've made up my mind. You're off the team. You'll be spending the afternoons at church."

"And if it means that I lose my chance?"

"Life isn't about one chance. If you miss this one, you'll have another. I know you don't believe that right now, but you're going to have to trust me. I have to do what I think is best, and this is it." I opened my mouth, but she shook her head, cutting me off before I could get out a word. "I'm going back to work."

She walked out of the room without another word. It seemed that there should be something else to mark the occasion. Thunder. Lightning. But there was nothing. It turns out when everything you've wanted in your life comes to an end, the only sound it makes is the click of the front door closing behind your mother.

22

God, in the Bible there's the story of Job. Apparently you and the devil had a bet that no matter how lousy you were to Job, he wouldn't turn against you. Then you proceeded to make his life a living hell. I'm thinking Job might have been some kind of slow learner, or else he was taking some kind of early Prozac, because he was way too mellow when his life was falling apart. I am not handling things nearly as well. If this is another bet with Satan, I should warn you that you might lose this round.

I stood in the cafeteria line, trying to breathe through my mouth so I didn't have to smell what they were serving. I had forgotten my lunch on the kitchen counter, which was just one more thing that was going wrong in my life. The long list of things going wrong.

"It could be worse," Joann said, giving her sock elastic a yank.

"How could it be worse? I'm off the track team and I have to spend my free time with Reverend Evers."

"Your mom could have grounded you from everything, not just track."

"What everything? It isn't like my social life is exactly brimming over these days."

"What about Todd?"

"What *about* Todd?"

"Nothing, I just thought maybe you guys would be hanging out." Joann didn't meet my eyes. She shuffled forward in line, looking out over the cafeteria.

"Why would you think that?"

"I don't know. Colin and I were talking about it, and he thought you guys would get along—you know, make a good couple."

"So now Colin is Mr. Relationship Expert?" I gave a snort.

"Well, don't be all mad at me, you asked." Joann stretched her neck, trying to see what the lunch ladies were serving. "Can you tell what they're having? I'm starving."

"You must be feeling better if you're hungry for anything they make here."

Joann stopped in line and looked me straight in the eye, her chin thrust up like a challenge.

"I went home yesterday and had the doctor check me out. I'm feeling fine now."

"Good." We stared each other down for a beat and then started shuffling forward again. So much for clearing the air on the passing-out issue. No wonder I have no social life, I can't even make it through a lunch period without ticking off my best friend. I tried changing the conversation.

"I heard you and Colin were nominated for the king and queen thing for the dance. That's cool."

"I know! I couldn't believe it. It never even occurred to me that we'd be nominated. Of course anyone can be nominated, it doesn't mean we'll make the court or anything."

"Well, you'll get my vote."

"Were you ticked?"

"About what?"

Joann's face went blank, her eyes wide. I've known her for far too long. There's no way she is even capable of keeping a secret.

"What would I be ticked about?" I asked again.

"It's nothing."

"Joann."

"I heard someone nominated you and Todd."

"Nice."

"I'm sure it was just a joke."

"Ha ha. The humor in this place kills me."

"Mr. Karp took your names off the list," Joann said.

"That hardly seems fair. What if we sweep the elections?"

"Todd can't win, he's suspended."

"Right. I'm sure that's all that is keeping me from the sash and crown."

The lunch lady dropped a glop of mystery casserole onto my tray. It was gray. I could think of no food product that was gray. The second lady put a spoonful of canned peaches in another section of the tray, topped it off with a slice of buttered Wonder bread, and passed it back to me. Ah, the lunch of champions.

I sat down at our table, but Joann was still standing, holding her tray.

"What's up?"

"Why don't we go over there?" Joann motioned toward a table near the window. Darci and her posse were sitting there, waving madly at Joann, as if this was wartime and Joann was their long-lost relative. I had my suspicions about who had nominated Todd and me.

"You go on ahead. I think I'm going to just grab a candy bar out of the vending machine or something."

"You sure?" Joann was already walking in their direction. She paused briefly to look back at me. I wanted her to sit with me without me having to ask her. I tried sending mental best friend psychic waves.

"Yeah. I'm not really hungry."

"Okay then—catch you later."

I watched her walk away. Darci and her friends all moved to the side to make room for her at the table and then closed ranks around her. No one else had gotten sick since Joann, or since Todd was suspended. Of course, no one was left to pass out anymore either. Well, no one except us losers.

I walked over to the garbage cans and dumped the tray over, watching my lunch slide into the trash.

23

God, people have been talking about the end of the world forever. There are tons of theories about when you're going to bring about the "big finish." Everything could be taken as a sign you're right around the corner and getting ready to kick ass and take names . . . but nothing happens. Times like now I almost wish you would come. Senior year isn't exactly panning out the way I had in mind, and it's possible the apocalypse might actually pick things up for me. I know that doesn't say much for my life.

It was only the third afternoon I had spent helping Reverend Evers and yet it felt like it had been, give or take, a thousand years. Todd hadn't called me, and since my mother had declared a fatwa on any social connection to Todd and was monitoring my every move, I couldn't reach him. Maybe Todd was mad that I'd run out after our kiss, without any explanation. I wanted to explain, but I wasn't sure how. Then again it's possible that Todd wasn't thinking about me at all, and that's why he didn't call. I wasn't sure which was worse; that it didn't matter to him or that he was pissed.

Spending afternoons at the church was like a time black hole where nothing changed and nothing moved forward. One afternoon I swear I saw the clocks running ever so slightly backward. Figures, the first real miracle in my life, and it's one that makes my life worse. The sad thing was that being at the church was the only real social interaction I was getting these days. Colin and I were back to acting like we hardly knew each other, and he was pulling the silent treatment on the whole Todd issue. He was the only one being silent; everyone else in school couldn't stop talking about Todd. Despite Officer Ryan's promise to Todd's family to keep the whole thing under wraps, everyone seemed to know every detail of his suspension and the details they didn't know they just made up. Never let truth get in the way of a really good story.

The tasks I had been given to do at church that, in theory, were going to make me a better person included all of the following: picking gum off the church steps, polishing the church pews, making copies of the song sheets for service, and weeding the front flower beds. It was not made clear how menial labor was supposed to shape my character. I could almost bear it except for the fact that Reverend Evers loved to sit in the church and discuss scripture while I did my chores. Actually, "discuss" is going too far. It implies he wanted any input from me. "Lecture" might be closer to what was happening. Although I have no proof, I strongly suspect that Reverend Evers makes Bible flash cards. He appears to have memorized the complete text. He could pull out a relevant quote for any subject, even subjects I'm pretty sure aren't covered in the Bible.

Today I was assembling baskets for the food bank in Van Wert. If poverty wasn't bad enough, I was noticing another problem. The baskets were full of crappy food: plain oatmeal, brown rice, cans of no-name tuna, and generic-brand bran flakes. The no-name tuna looked particularly shifty, like it might be made from regular-brand tuna leftovers, fins, scales, and eyeballs. Way too much fiber, way too little food with flavor. I would not have been shocked to see industrial-size containers of gruel.

"Maybe we should put some cookies or something in here," I said.

"These baskets are for the poor, Emma. They don't need dessert, they need sustenance. 'Charity suffereth long, and is kind; charity envieth not; charity vaunteth not itself, is not puffed up.' First Corinthians. This isn't about doing things that would make you feel better, this is about doing what needs to be done."

"Cookies are sustenance, and they aren't puffed up. I mean, I get that we shouldn't make up baskets full of junk food, but there isn't anything tasty in here."

I picked up another can of lima beans and put it in the basket. Lima beans? Does anyone actually eat those things? Maybe I could write it up: the canned lima bean poverty diet.

"The Lord helps those who help themselves. If we give people cookies, then they have no reason to work for them. It might seem as if it is nice, but remember the Lord wants us to teach people to fish, not give them fish."

"Giving the poor lima beans will inspire them to work harder?" This seemed like a dodgy theory to me. I have to think if it was that easy to wipe out poverty, someone else would have thought of it. Don't they have entire think tanks in Washington focused on solving these kinds of problems?

"In a way, yes. By giving people lima beans it inspires them to want for more and then to work for it. People need to learn values. Now, it's not a one-way street. We learn from the poor too. The poor provide us a chance to show charity."

"So you're saying God made some people poor so that those of us who aren't poor will learn to be kind?"

"Yes."

"That's sort of a rotten deal for the people born poor, isn't it?"

"The Lord works in very mysterious ways."

I was considering telling him there was mysterious and then there was downright twisted, when the phone rang.

Reverend Evers leaned back with a sigh. He likes his wife to answer the phone, and she was out for the day. I have the sense he feels the church should pay for a secretary. Answering the phone is beneath him. Unfortunately for him, Trinity Evangelical is not one of those giant churches seating a few thousand, with giant collection plates to match. There is no money in the church budget for a support staff. Perhaps the Lord was using this as an opportunity for those who had clerical support to learn charity, but I was pretty sure that Reverend Evers wouldn't appreciate this insight. I continued to pack the baskets, but pretty quickly it was becoming clear that something exciting was going on.

Reverend Evers had been seated behind his desk. It was huge, at least six feet long with carved legs and a million drawers. Entire rain forests may have been slaughtered to create this desk. If you ask me, no one needs a desk that big unless they have something to prove. The chair was just as fancy, burgundy leather, like a wingback chair on casters. I heard Reverend Evers make a surprised noise and I looked over to see him stand up as if he was at attention. He wasn't saluting, but he looked like he was ready to give it a try.

"Well, sir, I am very pleased to hear from you," Reverend Evers said.

He didn't look pleased, he looked ecstatic. He looked like how I imagine I would look if Prince William gave me a quick ring to see how I was doing and ask if I was interested in a trip to England. His one hand was holding the receiver and the other was fluttering at his side as if he might lift off, a giant six-foot hummingbird with a comb-over. I stopped even making a pretense of packing the baskets and listened.

"Indeed, it was disturbing. These children are our future." He nodded madly at whatever the person was saying on the line. "Why, I hadn't considered that. . . . No, I see the benefits, of course. . . . We would be most humbled, sir. . . . Why, when the ladies at the church council hear about this, they'll be just as pleased as punch. Tickled pink . . . Of course, Trinity Evangelical is my flock, not that I would want to glorify myself, of course, but I would want . . . really?" His face broke into a huge smile, as if the Publishers Clearing House folks had just pulled up and were hauling a giant cardboard check with his name on it up the front stoop. "And you have a name for the event? . . . Faith Forward? Why, I think that is lovely. The governor? Well . . . You know what the Bible says, 'And by thy sword shalt thou live, and shalt serve thy brother.' We'll begin preparations right away. My wife and I would of course welcome you to stay in our home. . . . No, of course I understand. We'll talk to you soon."

Reverend Evers placed the receiver down carefully as if it might explode. He stood still for a second and then began to pace back and forth behind his desk. He wrung his hands together.

"Everything all right?" I asked.

Reverend Evers turned to face me. His face had this wide smile, as if he had just had a religious vision. He threw his arms wide, and I feared for a second that he might fall to his knees.

This is how I came to be the second person in Wheaton to know that *Born-Again Today*, the TV show, was coming to town.

24

God, who am I to cast stones? But if you want a piece of advice, you might want to take a look down here and see who's talking about you. You've got quite a few people, in pretty much every far corner of the world, who proclaim they are tight friends with you and have the okay to speak on your behalf. Then they say some pretty foul things, and some of the things they do would curl that giant white beard you've got going. Trust me on this—when your own so-called friends start talking about you, you really develop a reputation.

Born-Again Today is hosted by Reverend Maxwell Teaks, also known as Miracle Max. My grandmother loves this show. I fully expect that when she dies we'll discover that she's signed over the family farm to him. Reverend Teaks is from the fire-and-brimstone revival style of preaching. The kind you see on cable channels early on Sunday mornings, with choirs singing away behind him and hordes of people swaying back and forth. He works himself up into a lather and cries out "Jee-zus." Heavy on the *z* sound. Then various people wander down the aisle to be healed. He places his hand on their heads and then sort of shoves them back. They either get better, in which case it's due to the good reverend (with help from the Lord, of course), or they don't, in which case the afflicted person's faith is found wanting. The world according to Reverend Teaks is pretty black and white. He doesn't view many issues as falling into a morally gray zone. The way he sees it, either it is right (thus sanctioned by God and the good reverend) or wrong (thus dooming the person in question to an eternity of twisting and burning like a kebob on a Weber grill).

Teaks has gotten himself into trouble here and there. His views aren't always popular. When there was a hurricane a few years ago, Reverend Teaks gave his opinion that the cities that took the hardest hit had to pay a price because of their loose morals. He said the cities wouldn't have been harmed if they hadn't condoned abortion, gays, and premarital sex. You would think if God wanted to take out some nudie bars and a pride parade he could be a bit more pointed in his destruction and not have to take out the whole city.

Now *Born-Again Today* was going to do a live show from right here in Wheaton. It was going to be a special called "Faith Forward" and would highlight how, with the help of faith, we were fighting "terror in the heartland." How exactly faith would stop the reign of terror wasn't exactly clear to me, but the details didn't appear to matter to anyone else. The cable channel was running ads that flashed shots of the Columbine killers, then Osama bin Laden, Saddam Hussein, the twin towers, and then a picture of the good reverend in front of a waving American flag. The event was growing too big to fit in the church, and it quickly became clear that it wouldn't work in the school gym, either. People from all over the state were signing up to come. A giant white tent was shipped up from Indianapolis, and the Hansen family donated one of their fields for the site. There were rumors that news agencies were going to come to town to cover the event. The governor of Indiana had already indicated that he was coming, and one of the ladies at Sheer Beauty told everyone that she had it on good authority that Larry King might show up.

The school band would supply the music for the event, and the TES church choir was practicing in overdrive. It was determined that with high-def TV, new choir robes would need to be ordered. Imagine the shame if Trinity Evangelical was on the national stage and people saw frayed cuffs, faded colors, and nappy velvet. Oh, the inhumanity.

This was the biggest thing to ever happen in Wheaton, and it was all anyone could talk about, including all the students in the TES cafeteria. All around me I could hear people oohing and aahing over the possibility of appearing on TV. It was like they expected Angelina Jolie to show up and adopt a Wheaton kid. I tried to eat my salad in peace and block out the craziness. Besides, I had bigger things to obsess about, like track. I had faith that if I kept my nose clean, my mom would buckle. She knew how much track meant to me. I had missed a meet on Wednesday, but I was hoping not to have to miss any others. She was making a point, and I was attempting to show I got it. While I waited for her to see the error of her ways, I was keeping up with my training regime so I would be ready when she caved. I tried to focus on visualizing the feeling of crossing the finish line.

Darci and her gang sat a table over, gushing over Reverend Teaks and his show, which I strongly suspected none of them even liked until they heard it was coming to town. Of course, now that being poisoned was yesterday's news, they needed something else to focus on, so why not media celebrity? Joann was sitting with them. She'd waved for me to join them, but I had held up my biology book, indicating I had to study. It seemed more polite than implying that close proximity to Darci would make my gag reflex kick in. I tried to focus on the exciting life of cell structure, but I could still hear them.

"My mother says I might have to take Friday off. She's going to take me into Fort Wayne to get my hair and nails done for the show," Darci said. She was sitting in the center of a cluster of girls, and I couldn't help but notice there were more around her than usual.

"At a salon?" a freshman said in awe, as if that was equal to the Promised Land.

"I'm going to have to sleep sitting up so I don't ruin my hair." Darci laughed. "A woman's hair is her crowning glory, you know."

I tried not to gag on a crouton.

"I can't believe you're going to be on national TV!"

"I know. My dad says the choir will do at least two or three songs during the show. Plus, since Kimberly and I were the first victims of the attack, Reverend Teaks will likely want to pray over us. Give us his blessing."

"Maybe you'll be discovered."

I gave a snort. Darci turned to face me.

"Is there a problem?" she said with a hair flip.

"It's *Born-Again Today*, not *American Idol*."

"Envy is a sin, you know," said Darci.

"Envy?" I rolled my eyes and started to pack my lunch away. Suddenly I wasn't hungry anymore. "The whole thing is a joke."

Darci stood up and blocked my path, crossing her arms in front of her. She looked over at the group to make sure she had the maximum audience.

"I'm not surprised you would think so. You've always stuck out here, and if you didn't have Joann keeping you company out of the kindness of her heart, you wouldn't have any friends at all."

Joann didn't meet my eyes. Instead she stared down at her square of pizza and tub of applesauce as if she had never seen them before.

"I don't like to be friends with people who are fake. So I might not have a ton of friends, but at least the ones I have are real."

"How interesting. All this talk about real, it makes me wonder what kind of friend you really are."

I looked at her. I felt the salad in my stomach do a roll-over. Self-tossing salad, not a good thing. I had the feeling she and Joann had discussed more than the spring dance when Darci was over. I had the feeling she knew about the infamous Christmas kiss. Joann had begged her mom not to tell anyone, and up until now I thought we had managed to keep the whole thing a secret. I shot another look at Joann, who was still pondering the mystery of her hot lunch with the kind of concentration shown by biohazard engineers.

"You shouldn't talk about things you know nothing about," I said.

"I know you were the only person I ever saw Todd talk to. I heard the two of you went for long drives out to the abandoned theater. We all know what he was capable of. I guess the only question is, what are *you* capable of?"

"Todd had nothing to do with any of this. Everyone seems to forget there haven't been any charges."

"The school hasn't charged him yet because they have to make sure the case is solid and that they have all his accomplices."

"Solid? There are no charges because there's no evidence. Despite what your dad would have people believe, video games are not really the tool of Satan."

"How sweet. Are you protecting your lover?" Darci drew out the last word, and a few of the younger girls gave a gasp. The accusation of fornication hung in the air. Anyone who hadn't been paying attention was turning around to see what was going on.

"You better watch your mouth, Darci Evers," I said. She sneered and turned back to her friends. "You get out to the Barn much these days?" I asked, matching her sneer.

Darci turned back slowly to face me. Her face was flushed red, and she was breathing in deep puffs like a dragon ready to go off into spouts of flame and smoke.

"What did you say?"

"I asked if you got out to the Barn." I snapped my fingers as if I had just remembered something. "Oh, that's right, you wouldn't go out to the Barn, what with all the things that go on out there. The parties, the drinking, I hear even drugs. Why, people could get themselves into real trouble out there. Lucky for us we have you to act as TES's personal role model."

As for what happened next, you could argue it was my own fault. I turned my back on an angry Darci.

25

God, I would like to argue that humility as a virtue is overrated and should not be confused with humiliation. I don't think that I'm better than other people. I really don't. Perhaps you could lay off on lessons designed to teach me humility. For example, the time I sat on those raspberries in my white capri pants and then walked around all day with a giant red target on my ass. There was no point to that. It was just cruel.

I've known Darci Evers since first grade. I thought I knew a lot about her.

- She has the world's largest hair scrunchie/ ribbon collection in the school, one to match every outfit. (And hello? Who wears scrunchies anymore?)

- She has underwear with the days of the week sewn on the butt. (She's not the kind of person to get all wild and crazy and wear a Wednesday on a Thursday.)
- She thinks she sings like an angel, but the truth is she should stick with lip-synching. (What can you expect from someone who considers Britney Spears her vocal mentor?)

The one thing I didn't expect was that Darci Evers was a dirty fighter. I didn't see her as the type to fight at all. Plunge a figurative dagger in someone's back, sure. Hire a hit man, possibly. But a fighter? I never saw it coming. I turned my back on her for a fraction of a second, and she sprang on me like a crazed, rabid weasel. Her pink nails wound their way in my hair, and she jumped onto my back with a squeal that would shatter glass. We hit the floor, my lunch went flying, and the cafeteria chairs spun out of our way.

"CATFIGHT!" someone yelled out.

Darci had ahold of my hair and she seemed intent on yanking it out in one big hunk. We rolled around on the floor amid the cheering and screaming. My face rolled past what I am pretty sure was a dollop of dropped sauerkraut, and I felt it end up in my ear. Darci's hand—scratch that, talon—came out and raked across my face.

"Let go of me," I yelled as I kicked, trying to take her shins out or at least roll over so that she wouldn't have me pinned down.

For someone who is supposed to be full of Christian love, Darci was quite the scrapper. She was doing her best to pound my head against the floor in some kind of deranged WWF move when the fight was broken up. I like to believe that if I hadn't been surprised, or if the fight had lasted longer, I would have come out on top in the end. However, I had been surprised, and the fight hadn't gone on very long, so Darci was the one who drew the most blood. I could tell my nose was bleeding, and there was a huge scrape on my knee. The crowd gave an appreciative gasp. I had the sense that if my fellow students had lived in earlier times they would have enjoyed such wholesome sports as bearbaiting or watching gladiators fight to the death.

The group around us parted. It was like the Red Sea on speed, only instead of Moses, Mr. Reilly was standing over us. He bent down and pulled Darci up and off of me by her skirt waistband. He stood her up and looked her over. Her hair was pulled out of her ponytail holder, there was a smear of blood across her upper lip, and a shiny string of spit hung from her lower lip. Her eyes had a wild and crazy Lindsay-Lohan-on-a-bender look to them. I noticed that Mr. Reilly did not help me to my feet. I scrambled to stand up by myself. I stuck my pinkie in my ear to try to dislodge the hunk of sauerkraut.

The sleeve of my shirt was torn, and my uniform skirt was twisted around. My head hurt, and I was afraid that when I looked in the mirror I would discover a giant bloody bald spot.

"Ladies. I am astonished and disgusted," Mr. Reilly said.

Darci promptly burst into tears. Mr. Reilly reached over and grabbed a stack of paper napkins from the table and gently passed them to her. He looked at me and shook his head. I wiped my nose with my sleeve and tried to straighten my skirt. I'm sure he would have handed me a napkin if he hadn't given all of them to Darci. Ha ha ha.

"Emma, I want you to go down to Mr. Karp's office."

"Me?" I looked around to see if anyone else was appalled. "She hit me. She attacked me."

Darci didn't disagree, but instead wailed louder. Kimberly stuck to her side like a tick. She led Darci away down the hall as if Darci was a tragic victim of random violence. Everyone in the cafeteria was doing their best to act as if they hadn't noticed a thing, suddenly very interested in the contents of their lunches. I looked at Joann, waiting for her to say something. She stood there staring at me like she had never seen me before.

"I am not going to have this discussion with you. I want you to go right now." Mr. Reilly pointed dramatically down the hall toward Mr. Karp's office. He looked like he was God pointing Adam and Eve out of the garden. Banished. I looked around, seeing if there were any friendly faces, but when no one met my eyes, I shuffled down the hall.

Considering that before last week I had never been to Mr. Karp's office, I was suddenly starting to earn a lot of frequent visitor points. While I waited for my turn to see him, the secretary took pity on me. She brought me some wet paper towels and a Kleenex before going for her own lunch. I blotted the blood off and gave my nose a big honk. The door to Mr. Karp's inner sanctum was closed. I could hear the murmur of voices through the wood. I wondered if he had already called my mother. Any hope I had of earning my way back onto the track team by keeping my nose clean wasn't going exactly according to plan. I was determined not to cry, though. I wouldn't. I stared straight ahead, focusing on counting how many cement blocks were in the far wall.

"Psst."

I turned around. I didn't see anyone. People wandered by in the halls, but no one seemed to be paying any attention to me at all.

"Psst."

Great, now I was hearing voices. I rubbed the side of my head. I wondered if I had some kind of brain injury. Darci had whacked my head pretty good against the floor. Maybe it had resulted in some kind of clot in my skull. While I sat there, my brain tissue could've been dying. I swore if I ended up as a drooling, voice-hearing blob I'd sue that Bible thumper, so help me God.

"Hey."

I turned around again, and this time I saw him. Colin was just outside the office, pretending to get a drink from the fountain.

"What happened?" he asked.

"Darci attacked me in the cafeteria."

Colin laughed, spraying water back into the fountain.

"It's not funny," I clarified, but he kept laughing.

"We need to talk. Meet me after school?" he asked.

"I can't. I have to go over to the church. My mom has me volunteering."

"How about I meet you there?"

26

God, I hope when you were a kid you weren't perfect all the time. I mean, you would have been the most annoying classmate ever. Everyone would be like, "Don't hang with that Jesus kid." It would have been a miracle if you made any friends at all, let alone twelve of them. No one likes someone who's perfect all the time. A couple of nice flaws might round you out. Of course, if you have too many flaws you can end up like me, with no friends at all.

The meeting with Mr. Karp went better than expected. There were no threats of expulsion or damnation, which made for a refreshing change. Instead, the focus seemed to be on understanding what was going on with me. I imagine Mr. Karp had been reading up on books that extol the virtues of understanding and reaching today's troubled youth. I suspect he'd been role-playing how to "get down

"Sure. What's up?"

"I'll explain later." Colin gave me a nod and then slipped down the hallway. He hadn't said anything to make me feel that way, but I had the sense that it was going to be bad news. Maybe it was just the way the day was going.

and rap" with teens. No doubt, with the official story being that Todd had been on the cusp of wiping out the student population, Mr. Karp was feeling the need to connect with those of us on the fringes. There were a lot of comments about how it must be hard for me to be from a single-parent home and how he deeply understood how it could be difficult to be outside of the popular group. He included (at no extra cost) a touching story of his own youth, where apparently he was called Mr. Potato. This cruel name appeared to be related to both the general size and shape of his head (frighteningly misshapen once you noticed it) and the fact that his parents were potato farmers. I think this story was meant to bond us, two different generations, both experienced at being losers.

The outcome of my second visit to Karp's office was that I would be let off with nothing more than a reminder that violence doesn't solve anything and a promise to speak directly with him if I found myself having problems in the future. It didn't look like he would call my mom, so if I could avoid developing a black eye, there was a chance she wouldn't find out about the situation at all.

When I left his office, lunch was over and classes had started. The halls were empty. I was pulling the things I needed out of my locker when I heard Darci talking about me. She and Kimberly were around the corner, headed in my direction. The last thing I wanted was another confrontation. I looked around, but the bathroom was too far to make a break for it, and there wasn't anywhere in the hallway to hide. This is why more international spy rings aren't based in high schools—no dark corners. I did the only thing that made sense. I stepped into my locker and pulled the door shut.

I had to hunch down a bit to fit in below the shelf, and based on the fact that my ass was wedged in pretty tightly, I needed to step up my training program. I could just make out slivers of Darci's and Kimberly's faces through the vent as I peered out.

"Is my lip swelling?" asked Darci.

"A bit, but it doesn't look bad. Sort of sexy puffy," Kimberly offered.

"I totally hope Karp kicks her right out of school. She is not TES material."

"Do you think she knows? I mean, why else would she bring up the Barn?"

"There's nothing to know," Darci said, her voice firm. "She's just fishing around."

"But what about—"

"There is nothing to know. Do you understand me? Todd Seaver is responsible for what happened and that's it."

"But if he gets in real trouble, I mean, if it goes beyond the school or anything, then we would say something, right?"

"If Todd gets himself in the kind of trouble where the police get involved, then I guess he's in trouble. It has nothing to do with me."

"Is that a sin? I mean, to let him take the blame? He didn't really do anything."

"If God wants him to stay out of trouble, then he will."

"Do you think?"

"Well, of course. So what are you going to wear for the show?"

"Whatever we wear won't show because of the choir robes."

"Well duh, but you'll know what you're wearing. Besides, what if Reverend Teak asks us to sit down and chat with him while the cameras are on? I heard my dad saying they may do a segment with the students affected, and, let's be honest, who are they going to put up there? Kelly? I don't think so. They'll pick us."

I listened to their voices disappear down the hallway. I had the sense not only that Darci was completely capable of letting Todd take the blame, but, even scarier, that she had convinced herself that it had happened the way she imagined it. She wasn't the kind of person to let something pesky like the truth be a barrier to what she wanted.

I pushed on the door. I wanted out of there.

The door didn't move.

I gave it another push. There was no handle on the inside of the door. Clearly, they didn't design lockers for the person who might be on the inside. I rattled the door, but I was getting a sinking feeling. The lock must have clicked shut when I pulled the door closed. I gave the door yet another rattle and shove in case it thought I was just joking around. Maybe the locker needed to be shown who was boss.

Shit.

Locked inside my own locker. Never let it be said that God doesn't have a sense of humor. I heard the bell ring, and the hall filled with everyone rushing back and forth to class. I figured I had two choices:

1. Call out for help and always be known as the girl who locked herself in her own locker.
2. Slowly starve to death and be found a mummified corpse at the end of the year.

This was going to be a difficult decision. I didn't want to die, but added humiliation wasn't sounding too good either, especially coming on the heels of the lunch brawl. I decided

I would wait until the hallways cleared out, and sooner or later a teacher or janitor would walk by. There was no need for me to out myself in front of the entire student body of TES. The bell rang again and the hallways emptied. Any minute now someone would walk by. Any minute.

Okay, ten minutes had gone by and a few problems had come up (or should I say additional problems, since I still had the whole locked-in-the-locker crisis in action):

- I was developing a nasty kink in my neck from being in this odd crouched position. My muscles could lock up this way and I would be known as Ol' Hunchback for the rest of the year, and you never see hunchbacks winning track meets.
- I had an itch on my ankle, which I couldn't reach, and as a result it was driving me insane. I also had this fear that it might be a bug crawling on me, and I couldn't look down to check.
- The smell combination of my used gym gear and my lunch sack from yesterday was becoming decidedly unpleasant.
- I had to pee.

The last problem was the most pressing and potentially most damaging. It had now occurred to me that there was something worse than having the entire student body of TES know I locked myself in my locker. Having the entire student body of TES know I locked myself in my locker and then peed myself would be much worse. I tried to shift around, doing the bathroom dance, but it wasn't the easiest maneuver in the space provided.

"Uh, hello?" I called out through the vent. Nothing. "Little help here?"

I leaned my head back. It was going to be a race between the next bell, which would bring help, and the chance that I would end up peeing in my uniform, in which case I would have to quit school and join the Peace Corps. My lunch sack was hanging right at the side of my face, which also wasn't making the smell situation much better.

Wait a minute! I had a knife in my bag to spread peanut butter on my apple. I could use the knife to pry open the lock. I gave a whoop. I felt very Nancy Drew for coming up with a solution.

I squirmed so my hands were faceup at waist level and then, using the side of my head, I knocked my lunch sack off the hook. I caught the bag and fumbled with the Velcro closure. Why is it that in time of great need, Velcro

becomes the superglue of adhesives? I finally got the bag open and found the knife, although my bag of pretzels fell to the floor, where I promptly stepped on them. If something had to be sacrificed, I was willing to let the pretzels go. I got the knife into the lock and started to pry open the latch.

God? If you are there, I know I have prayed for some odd things in my life. If I had known I was wasting valuable prayer time on things like wanting to get boobs and hoping for a computer in my room, I wouldn't have done it. This time, God, I really need you. Now, I know you might be thinking that I don't deserve a miracle. I'm sure there are starving kids in Africa who deserve access to clean water more, or perhaps an old lady who is about to step out in front of a bus or something, but if you could spare me just a touch of miracle magic to get me out of this locker, I promise to try and be a better person. I'll never kiss any of my friends' boyfriends again.

Click.

The locker door swung open, and I fell out into the hallway. A freshman was standing a few lockers down, and I startled him so much he dropped his hall pass. I'm pretty sure he thought I was going to strap on a Superman cape and fly out of there as if my locker were a telephone booth.

I hopped up and brushed myself off, kicking the pretzel crumbs out of my way.

"What are you looking at?" I asked, and he scurried off, looking over his shoulder at me like he was scared I'd go chasing after him. I grabbed my bag and bolted for the girls' room.

Locker 0, God 1.

27

God, I don't get your stand on miracles. There are all these people who claim you've worked miracles, curing them of cancer or waking them from a coma, but it's been pointed out to me that you never help amputees. How hard would it be for you to grow someone a new leg? What do you have against amputees? If it's hard to restore a limb, maybe you could start with something small, like someone who has cut off a pinkie finger. And then there is your choice of who gets a miracle and who doesn't. Is there a complicated application system? Is it random? And if it's random, what's the point of praying in the first place? As long as we're on the topic of miracles, I could use another. Turns out we're having a test in U.S. history. With all that has been going on, it seems to have slipped my mind. It was in there at one point; I've read the chapters. If you could just find out what corner of my brain the answer is in and push it toward the front, it would be greatly appreciated.

I tapped my pen on the side of my leg and glanced around the room. Everyone had their heads down as they worked on their tests. I could hear Joann's pen scribbling away behind me. It was clear she hadn't forgotten to study.

Joann and I were doing our best to ignore what happened at today's lunch. Since Todd was ignoring me by not calling, I was doing my best to pretend the whole kissing thing hadn't happened either. This would be easier if I could simply stop thinking about it, but it was on some kind of weird loop in my head. If my brain was a TiVo, it was stuck permanently on Todd. I looked over at where Todd would normally have been sitting. His desk was empty, and although I know it made no sense at all, I wanted to slide a few rows over and sit in his seat, maybe put my head down on the desk. Of course, at the moment I wanted to be doing anything but this test.

The test was classic Mrs. Larramie. While other teachers might give you a nice multiple-choice test (often with one answer being absurdly wrong so you could eliminate it right away, giving you a fighting chance), Mrs. Larramie gave essay exams. There were usually only two or three questions, which meant you also weren't safe with skipping one and counting on hitting the others out of the park.

Mrs. Larramie felt it was her personal mission to prepare us for college. She thought high school kids had become soft and intellectually lazy. Every year she gave her classes the same speech at the beginning of the year about how things were when she went to school. She made it sound like she attended some kind of Third World school, where they had to make their own pens by whittling trees down with their teeth and use their own blood as ink. For some reason, she made this sound like it was a good thing. Apparently, in what she called the good old days, kids weren't spoon-fed education. In her day, kids had a passion for learning, and if they didn't, then they failed. The ones who failed were cursed to spend the rest of their lives as garbage collectors. In her day, kids did their own thinking, blah, blah, blah.

The first question on the test was, "Please detail the public opinion and level of support toward the Civil War in both the North and South. How did public opinion differ? How did the public reaction shape the government policy, and how does this compare to U.S. policy during the Iraq war?"

I was screwed, and then I got a miracle.

There was a knock at the classroom door, and the class spun around to face it. Mr. Karp was there, with Officer Ryan standing next to him like his personal bodyguard, ready to take any of us down in case we rushed him.

"Hi, Daddy!" Kimberly said with a small wave. Officer Ryan gave a big smile and one of those little-kid bye-bye waves by opening and closing his fist.

I slunk down in my chair. Just when I thought the day couldn't get any worse, I was about to be dragged away to the gulag. On the upside, any jail cell would be larger than my locker.

"Can we see Dwight Handle, please?" Mr. Karp asked. I sat up straighter. They weren't there for me.

Everyone turned to face Dwight, who looked as surprised as we did. Dwight is one of those kids where it's surprising he's survived high school up to this point. He is painfully thin. He looks like the Olsen twins' long-lost brother. He's always reading one of those eight-inch-thick fantasy novels with covers that have dragons and women with huge hooters holding giant phallic swords. Dwight also has an acne issue. I'm being nice; it's more than an issue. I'm not sure he has an inch of clear skin. I'm sure someday he will grow up to be some kind of brilliant computer scientist and make a zillion dollars a year, and most likely his skin will clear up too, but for now he's a loser. Acne—the leprosy of high school.

Throughout our years at TES, Dwight has been the

guy the jocks picked up and carried by the back of his underwear. Once they somehow managed to throw him up into the basketball hoop, and he was stuck there until the janitor could get him down. They used to shove him into his locker. (I have new sympathy for this problem.) Basically, Dwight is one of those kids who scurries around the corners of the hallways and no doubt is counting the days until the end of school. Now suddenly the school administration was coming for him.

Dwight stood up. I could see his Adam's apple bounce up and down as he swallowed. He gathered his things and shuffled out of the classroom. The room broke into whispers and Mrs. Larramie tried to get us back under control, but everyone was in gossip overdrive.

"All right! Everyone, pencils down," Mrs. Larramie bellowed. Pencils down? Did she think anyone was still working on the exam? "Pass your papers to the front. We'll reschedule the exam for tomorrow, but mark my words: I'll be making it harder, to reflect the fact that you'll have an additional night to study."

The exam was being rescheduled? Oh, beautiful miracle.

"I want everyone to pull out their books and start reading the next chapter. I'll be right back." Mrs. Larramie stood up and tugged her industrial gray cardigan down (she had boxy dressing perfected and always looked vaguely square shaped to me.) With one final disapproving glare, she marched into the hallway. Four seconds passed when everyone pretended to read about the carpetbaggers and the difficulty with the postwar restoration, and then the room erupted in whispers. I spun around to face Joann.

"Holy shit! Why would Karp take Dwight away?" I asked.

"It's not just Dwight. Joe Schneider's in trouble too," Joann said.

"And Carla Gangon," added Paula, joining our conversation. She was sitting on the edge of her chair, her eyes wide and her face flushed with excitement.

"Carla?" I asked. Her name didn't ring any bells to me.

"Everyone calls her 'Carla Gag-on,'" Paula clarified. "The really fat sophomore girl?"

Suddenly I knew exactly who she was talking about. I'd never talked to her, but Carla either had some kind of really unfortunate gland issue or consumed enough food for a family of four. She moved through the hallways like a giant ocean tanker.

"I didn't know about Carla," Joann whispered. "I never imagined."

"Imagined what?" I asked.

"You paying attention, Proctor? Gag-on must have been part of the group that was planning to bring down the school," Paula said. "I heard the parent advisory board did a full investigation and are hunting down all the people who could have been involved."

"They think Dwight was involved?" I asked.

"I heard they're looking at all the losers who have, like, no friends and hate it here."

"Are you serious?"

"Yeah. Do you think they're just going to let these people stay in class? What if they go postal like Todd?"

"So, what . . . ? They're going to take them off and shoot them instead?"

"Maybe they'll go to some kind of loser re-education camp," Paula offered.

"What makes them think these guys are a threat?" I asked.

"You seem awfully concerned about what happens to them," Paula noted.

"Come to the bathroom with me," said Joann. Suddenly she was on her feet, dragging me behind her. Once we were in the hallway, she turned around and faced me. I was surprised to see she was angry.

"What is the matter with you?" she hissed.

"What are you talking about?"

"All of a sudden you're every loser's personal defense attorney?"

Shocked, I could only stare at Joann.

"Losers?" I asked, and her face flushed.

"I didn't mean losers. I just meant it's a bunch of people we're not even friends with. Ever since this whole thing started, you seem to be on their side."

"There are sides?"

"Of course there are sides. You can think whatever you want, but people have gotten sick. Someone's responsible, and the school did find stuff in Todd's locker."

"You mean like when you got sick? Someone is responsible for that?"

Joann looked down at her shoes. There was no way I was going to believe Joann had passed out. She was many things, but a frail, passing-out flower type was not one of them.

"If it was just me, that would be one thing, but it's happened to a lot of people."

"Lucky for me, just the popular people."

"You could be popular if you wanted. You always act like you're better than the popular crowd, like you're above the whole thing. There's nothing wrong with wanting to have friends."

"You mean the kind of friends who stick up for you if you're in a fight, for example."

Joann took a step back as if I had struck her.

"Everything happened so fast. Reilly broke it up before I knew what happened."

"Innocent people could get into a lot of trouble if everyone starts blaming other people for no reason," I said, changing the subject.

"Anyone who's innocent will be able to prove it."

"If this town doesn't string them up before they *can* prove it. You know how it is, things can happen fast."

"People are talking about you, you know."

"Talking about me?" I crossed my arms and leaned back against the lockers. "Oooh, how will I go on if people are talking about me? Oh, the horror."

"Be a smartass if you want. People are talking about how you never got along with a lot of the popular girls who got sick, how you started hanging out with Todd, how you talk about hating it here. And then there's the fact that you sometimes make fun of God."

"Make fun of God? What's the matter, did I hurt his feelings?"

"See, it's flip stuff like that. It makes you look un-Christian. It seems like your personal relationship with Jesus is just a joke."

"How does anyone know what the hell my personal relationship with Jesus is like? That's the whole point; it's personal. How is it that people feel comfortable skipping over parts in the Bible like, 'Don't judge others,' but feel more than welcome talking about how well they know the book?"

"Do you even believe?" Joann asked, her voice getting louder.

I gave a sigh. How did this turn into a fight? I didn't even like Dwight, and I didn't know Carla, and all of a sudden my best friend and I were going at it and the guy I did like was ignoring me after I basically lip mauled him in his kitchen. Things were out of control. How I was supposed to know how to answer questions about my faith?

"I don't know," I said softly. The answer surprised me almost as much as Joann.

"What?"

"I don't know what I believe anymore. It's not a sin to have doubts. Do you ever wonder why you believe? Think about it. Religion is an accident of geography. If you had been born in Israel, odds are you would be Jewish. In Japan? Buddist. Iran? Muslim. Don't you ever wonder if everything we've been told really makes sense?" I grabbed her arm. Suddenly I wanted—no, I needed—to talk to Joann. I wanted to lie on her pink bedspread and tell her everything that had been swirling around in my mind. I wanted to have a good cry with my best friend. She yanked her arm back.

"I can't believe you're saying this. Colin and I have been sticking up for you."

"I never asked you to stick up for me, and I sure as hell didn't ask Colin to be involved."

"When people started hinting around that you might be involved in all of this too, I told them no way, but now I feel like I don't even know you anymore."

"I'm the same person I've always been. Even if I didn't believe, it would still be okay. Well, except for here in Wheaton."

We stood in the hall facing off, neither of us saying anything.

"Then I guess you should get out of Wheaton."

"Don't be mad," I said.

"I'm not mad."

"Yes, you are, your ears are all red. I've known you forever. Your ears always get red when you're ticked," I pointed out, hoping to make her laugh. Maybe she needed to be reminded that she didn't need more friends, she had me.

"You've known me forever, but I guess the question is, do I want to know you anymore?" Joann spun around and walked back into the classroom without saying another word. I wondered how many people in the classroom had been listening in. I'm guessing give or take the entire crowd. At this rate it was going to be just a matter of time until Officer Ryan showed up looking for me. I thought about Todd and wondered how he was doing. In some ways I was glad my mom had forbidden me to talk to him. I could only imagine what he would think of someone keeping quiet while other people took the blame. I nibbled on the corner of my thumbnail and remembered how he had pointed out the stars.

The whole thing was falling apart. I needed to talk to Colin. It was time for us to come clean before anyone else got dragged down.

28

God, if you're out there and still speaking to me despite the fact that I've admitted to a few doubts, I could use some help. My best friend hates me, my best friend's boyfriend likes me, and the guy I kissed happens to be someone who everyone thinks is a serial killer—and he isn't speaking to me anymore since I ran out on him. I'm pretty sure not speaking is going to put a real cramp in any future relationship we may have. Or are all these things happening because *I had some doubts? Is this supposed to drive me back to the fold? I'm thinking a softer approach would work better.*

Reverend Evers was in a cleaning lather. There are people with serious cases of OCD who wash their hands until they bleed who are not as clean-focused as the reverend had been lately. He knew the eyes of the world were going to be on Trinity Evangelical, and he was going to do his part to make sure Wheaton didn't let them down. While the world was pondering what a near miss we had of terror in the heartland, he was going to ensure they also noticed our clean and tidy community. He forced the Sheer Beauty salon to get rid of all their tabloid magazines (false idols), and the gas station had taken down the sign they'd had up forever that said GOT GAS? He thought the sign hinted at a fart joke, which he felt was beneath us. Or at least beneath what we wanted people to think we were, like when you clean the house for company and stuff everything in the closet. It is less important to be clean than to have people *think* that you're clean. When Wheaton hit the TV airwaves, we were going to be a perfect town (or at least give the appearance of perfection), and he was going to be the heart of the whole thing.

Lucky for the good reverend, he had me as his own personal slave labor to assist with his endless to-do list. I briefly considered telling him the truth, that the whole "terror in the heartland" was really little else than a case of rural girls gone wild. I opened my mouth to tell him, but before I said a word, I knew he wasn't going to listen. He wouldn't believe me, because then there wouldn't be the TV show and it would mean his daughter was a liar. We hadn't grown too close over the past few days, but I was fairly sure this was the kind of news that wouldn't go over well.

If I was going to do this, I had to do it right. My best option would be to convince Colin to go with me to talk to my mom and take it from there. She might not believe me, but she would believe Colin. Maybe he'd had the same realization, which is why he wanted to meet.

I was outside putting a fresh coat of white paint on the church sign. I had been painting only ten minutes and had already managed to get paint on my nose and on my new jeans. I stood there staring at the blotch of white paint on my pants and wondered if there was any way to travel back in time a few seconds and tell myself not to lean on the sign. I touched the sticky paint. If I went into the bathroom and took off my pants, could I wash it out before it dried? Or would that make it worse? Was this one of those things where if you knew the secret laundry trick, it would come right out, but if you didn't, it would set forever and even a jackhammer wouldn't get it off? Maybe I could single-handedly bring back the eighties fashion of paint-splattered jeans. Puff up my hair, play some Duran Duran.

I turned around when I heard a car pull into the church parking lot. It was Colin. He sat in his truck for a few moments before getting out and heading over to me. Colin never walks anywhere. He has this sort of lope. I used to wonder if he had one leg shorter than the other and that's what caused it, but it seems to be just his nature. He doesn't move along as much as he slowly bounces along.

"You're doing it wrong," he said, as he got closer.

"I'm putting paint on the sign. How can it be wrong as long as there is paint?"

"You've got too much paint on the brush. The idea is to do as many coats as you need, but to build the paint up one layer at a time, not slap it up in one thick coat."

"One thick coat is much more efficient." I held the brush out to him. "Want to show me how it's done, Mr. Home and Garden Network? You're so much better at this stuff than me."

He took the brush from me and stepped up to the sign. I sat down on the grass and took a drink from my water bottle. With my other hand, I brushed the hair out of my eyes. Shit. Now I had paint in my hair, too. Colin looked down at me and gave a laugh.

"Don't think you're so clever. I know you're just being nice so I'll paint the sign for you," he said.

"Flattery will get a girl everywhere. I'm glad you came by. We need to talk," I said.

"I know. There's something I want to tell you." Colin was concentrating on the sign and not looking at me.

"Why do I have the sense this is bad news?"

"It's not good or bad."

"Okay, hit me."

Colin reached into his pocket, pulled out a crumpled-up envelope, and tossed it down on the ground next to me. I looked at it.

"I was in the athletic office today. I had to pick up a medical form for my little brother. I saw that on Attley's desk and swiped it."

I unfolded the letter. It was from Northwestern University. They were sending a scout to see me at the next meet. A scout! I scanned the letter. It didn't say if they had settled on an amount for my scholarship, but if they were sending someone out to see me, they must be thinking full ride. They wouldn't bother sending a scout all the way to Middle of Nowhere, Indiana, if all they planned to do was give me a few bucks to cover my books.

I gave a whoop and then did a series of cartwheels across the churchyard, the letter clutched in one hand. I didn't even care that I had paint on my jeans. From this moment forward, whenever I saw the jeans I would remember how I was wearing them the day I got the news. Then it hit me. I wasn't on the track team anymore, and I was planning on sharing information that would make sure

I never got back on. I stopped midcartwheel and slumped to the ground.

"You okay?" Colin called out. I sat in the middle of the yard, looking at the letter. The seal of the university was in the corner in thick, dark purple ink. It was raised a bit, and I ran my fingers over it like it was Braille. I walked back to Colin and sat down. He was still painting the sign.

"I'm screwed," I said finally.

"No, you're not. The track meet is Saturday morning, and the Faith Forward show isn't being taped until the afternoon. You can go to both."

"This isn't about that stupid show!"

"Easy. I was yanking your chain. Joann told me you're grounded and your mom is making you take a break from the track team. What you need to do is throw yourself on her mercy, and I bet she'll let you run. Attley will let you on the team for sure. You're his star racer."

"That's not my problem." I looked up at him. "Have you heard about Todd and what's happening with the other kids?"

"Yeah. Karp came for Stu Hills in my biology class."

"Stu? Boo-Boo Stu?" I asked. Stu had earned the unfortunate nickname due to the fact that he was near terminally clumsy. I used to wonder if he had an inner ear disorder that threw off his balance. Once he walked into a low bookshelf in the library and needed twenty-eight stitches. He fell down stairs, tripped over things like dust, fell off chairs, and generally was a walking disaster waiting to happen. If I got onto a plane and saw Boo-Boo Stu sitting there, I would get off, because that would be the plane whose engine would fall off. He has that kind of luck.

"I don't think they're kicking them out of school, just taking them in for questioning."

"What did you think about Joann passing out?"

Colin shrugged.

"It didn't bother you?"

"She felt sick. It's no big deal. She's not saying anyone did anything to her."

"This whole thing is so crazy," I said.

"I know."

"We have to tell somebody what we saw."

"If you tell, there's absolutely no way you can run in the meet on Saturday."

I noticed that the "we" had turned into a "you." I felt my stomach tighten up.

"I guess if I told I'd be screwed, huh?"

Colin shrugged and kept painting, not saying a word.

"So you want to keep quiet about the whole thing?" I asked.

"I thought that was your big plan."

"That was before they started dragging people off."

Colin rolled his eyes. "Dragging people off? You're starting to give Darci the drama queen a run for her money."

"Okay, they're not dragging them off, but they're getting into trouble."

"They're getting themselves into trouble."

"What are you talking about?"

"The way I heard it is that they questioned Joe and he was the one who gave them Carla and Dwight's names. Dwight apparently gave them Stu's name."

"That doesn't make any sense."

"My guess is, if you want to get out of trouble you point the finger at someone else."

"I bet Darci started the whole thing."

"Probably."

"This situation is seriously fucked up," I offered.

Colin continued painting in tight, measured strokes. He worked with precision, like he was defusing a bomb, not painting a stupid church sign. For some reason this made me want to yank the brush out of his hand and start flinging paint around.

"Besides, you don't really care about the situation," he said, darting a quick look in my direction. "Why don't you admit the reason you're thinking of telling is because Todd is in trouble?"

"Todd and everybody else."

"You want me to believe you really care what happens to Boo-Boo?"

"I like Stu."

"No, you like Todd."

I crossed my arms over my chest and stared at Colin until he stopped painting and looked at me.

"Is that what this is about? You're mad that I like Todd instead of you."

"So you admit you like him."

"Oh my God. Can you hear yourself? This situation is *so* not about you or me or who we're going out with or not going out with."

"I get it. Todd doesn't like you." Colin's mouth tipped up in a small smile, and I fought the urge to smack the smile right off his face. I was developing rage issues. I could feel layers of my stomach lining being slowly eroded by acid.

"What are you talking about?"

"Is that how you're going to win his love? Deliver him

safely from the clutches of Officer Ryan and the torch-burning locals?"

I could feel my nostrils flare out, but that wasn't the annoying part. The annoying part was the feeling that I was about to start crying. My throat felt hot and raw and I could tell my lower lip was doing that pre-cry shake. Colin, who has known me forever, spotted the signs right off the bat.

"Hey," he said softly. He balanced the brush on the top of the paint can and then reached over to touch my arm. "I was just joking around."

"I'm not thinking about telling just because of Todd, it's because of everyone. And because I'm sick of Darci getting away with whatever she wants." I left off the part where it was mostly about Todd.

"I didn't come to fight over all of this. Sit down with me." Colin took me by the elbow and led me away from the paint. We plunked down, our knees touching. I heard a car round the corner and pulled away slightly. All I needed was someone, say Joann's mom, for example, to drive by and see us sitting together. I ran my palm over the top of the grass. Colin reached into his pocket and pulled out a small box and flicked it open. Inside was a gold ring, with a thin band and a tiny diamond sliver. I sat straight up.

"Holy shit!" I pushed the ring away as if he had opened

/e were friends, good friends,
›uld be together. Did he think
ıtion and a *ring* was going to

aid, pulling the ring back. My
azing I didn't choke, what with
· in there.
"

ement ring, either; the sales clerk
an't afford a proper engagement
ring a quick once-over and put it
oing to give it to Joann. I wanted
lin stared off into the distance to
say was being held up by giant cue
ke it was the kind of thing I needed
her. I hope you'll keep it a secret."
n's talking to me right now, so it
I suddenly felt like I should be doing
up, brushed off my jeans, and went

few more strokes. The paint dripped
g white splotches on the ground. "I
What happened to what you said to

on what
said you
getting
doesn't
wo sec-
."
ough I
e caus-
you. It
tem or
u and
de off
se to
s I'm
ably

me, about how you didn't want us to miss out could have been. To have our big chance?"

"What chance are you talking about? You didn't like me that way."

"Well as long as you aren't having trouble over it."

"So now you don't want me to be happy?"

"Of course I want you to be happy, but that mean I want you to get engaged to someone else t onds after I tell you."

"It's not an engagement ring, it's a promise ring

"Fuck your promises." I kept painting, even t couldn't see clearly. Stupid paint fumes seemed to b ing my eyes to water up.

"I'm sorry. I never should have said anything to was a mistake. Something I had to get out of my sys something."

"Well, that makes me feel better. So the plan is y Joann will graduate and have a summer wedding? R into the sunset together?"

"No, I don't have a plan. I'm making a prom Joann to show I intend to stick it out. So she know serious about waiting while she's in school. We pro won't get married for a few years."

"So you'll just hang out keeping the cows company until she graduates?"

"Ha ha. There's nothing wrong with not going to college, you know. I'm going to take some business classes, but I'm going to focus on the farm. My dad and I are working out a deal where he'll sign it over to me in a few years."

"And that's really what you want?"

"And that's what I want." Colin stood up. "I should get going. I just thought you should know. Just something one friend might tell another." He started to walk toward the parking lot.

"Wait a minute." I put the brush down. "We need to decide what to do about the other thing. I still think we should tell."

"What's the point? The whole thing will blow over in a few weeks."

"Not for the people getting hassled. It's not going to be over for them in a few weeks. As long as they live in this town, people are going to look at them funny."

"I don't want to tell. There's nothing to be gained. They're blaming each other. That's not my fault. I don't need the hassle."

"Oh, you don't want to be bothered if it means people will be pissed at you? Excuse me, I mean the right people. It doesn't matter if the kids on the outside get screwed."

"And this has nothing to do with Todd being one of the people in trouble?"

"Yes, fine, I like Todd," I said. "But don't act like this isn't about what you think is best for you. You don't want Joann to know you were with me and that you know her whole pass-out thing is a bunch of bull. Sort of makes your promise look pretty shallow."

"Whatever. I gotta go." Colin looked over at the sign. "You're still using too much paint."

I hurled the paintbrush after his back, but it missed him by a mile and landed with a soft *whump* in the grass. He turned to face me.

There was still one more thing I had to know. "You brought over the letter about the scholarship as a bribe, didn't you?" I asked quietly. "A way to make sure I keep my mouth shut, right? Should I consider it a lovely parting gift?"

"Take it any way you want. What I think doesn't matter. But if you want my opinion, it makes way more sense for you to keep your mouth shut. Convince your mom to let you run in the race, and then you get exactly what you want."

"What's that?"

"A ticket out of town."

29

God? Are you there? And if you are, are you paying any freaking attention to what is going on? I have to be honest here, and please take this in the nicest way possible, but I'm starting to have some real doubts about you. Either you don't exist, or you do exist and your decisions are completely random. I used to think the idea of no God was the scariest thing I could imagine, but I'm thinking the idea of you around without any kind of plan is even scarier. Consider this advice: Pull up your socks.

After Colin left, I thought I would burst into tears. I've set new crying records in the past couple of weeks, but strangely enough, this time the tears didn't come. It was like I had finally run out. I finished painting the sign and took a step back. It didn't look right. The paint was sort of blobby in spots, and I had spilled paint on the grass below. Screw it.

I washed up and left without saying a word. If I had run into the reverend, either he would have noticed that I was upset, in which case he would have wanted to have a long and meaningful discussion about it, or he wouldn't have noticed, in which case he would have wanted to give me more things to do. So I washed up the paintbrushes and slipped out of the church.

I was glad my mom wasn't home. I wanted the place to myself, although I wasn't really sure what I wanted to do. Kicking something came to mind. Colin felt like a reasonable option. I paced back and forth in my bedroom, giving Mr. Muffles, my stuffed dog, a lecture on what a backwater hellhole we lived in.

I snatched up the phone and called Todd's house. His mother picked up the phone. I opened my mouth but couldn't think of what to say. I could hear his mother sounding like she was very far away instead of just across town, calling out hello. Then she snapped.

"These prank calls have to stop. You people can't just keep calling here and hanging up. We have caller ID. I'm writing all these numbers down!" She hung up the phone.

Great. My first attempt to reach out, and Todd's going to see my number on the harassing calls list. Things just kept getting better all the freaking time.

The afternoon was hot, one of those spring days where

summer is breathing down your back. I propped the window open, but there wasn't much of a breeze. I unfolded the paper from Northwestern and read it again and again. I felt like I was trapped in one of those Choose Your Own Adventure books, only I knew there wasn't any option for peeking ahead or doing it over if I didn't like how things panned out. I flopped down on my bed with a notebook and tried to rationalize the situation.

Tell on Kimberly and Darci

Pros:

- Keeps anyone else from being sucked into this situation (added bonus: could make T-shirts that say "Free Boo-Boo Stu," which has a cult status kind of sound).
- Would clear Todd's name, and he may be grateful enough that he would speak to me again and possibly give the kissing thing another shot.
- Would prevent Darci and Kimberly from appearing on national TV, except for potentially a segment on FOX News called "Christian Teens Gone Bad."
- Has that general "right thing to do" feeling.

Cons:

- Bye-bye track team and any chance at a full ride.
- Further alienates me from any of my friends (not that I wasn't doing a fine job of that all on my own) and will result in me being the town pariah, a situation that will possibly be made worse by eliminating my ticket out of town, thus leaving me trapped here for years.
- There is the real chance that no one will believe me, thus resulting in my being a town pariah without any of the pros.

Keep my Mouth Shut

Pros:

- Most likely with proper apology could convince Mom to let me run in track meet, thus providing a way out of town.
- No one hates me (any more or less than they already do).
- Everyone likes the story more than they will like the truth.

Cons:

- Todd and the others may be run out of town by hostile locals. (Nothing against the others, but what upsets me the most is the idea of Todd taking the blame for it all.)
- If Todd is run out of town, and it is partly my fault, it is unlikely he will want to attempt any type of romantic relationship with me.

I kept going back and forth, trying to figure out what to do. It felt like my brain was spinning on a hamster wheel without making any progress. I rolled over and curled around Mr. Muffles. The sun was shining in the window, and every so often the curtain gave a halfhearted ripple from the faint breeze. Then I fell asleep.

There is something about falling asleep in the late afternoon. You tend to have the same kind of dreams you do when you have a high fever, very vivid and very weird. This dream was no different.

In the dream I was walking around a city. It was one of those cities that can exist only in a dream. It seemed to be part Chicago, a dash of New York, and I'm pretty sure I saw the Eiffel Tower, too. In the dream this makes perfect sense somehow and doesn't bother me. I'm walking around the city, and I know I'm supposed to be someplace. I'm a little late and a lot lost. I keep asking people for directions, but no one seems to want to help me. Then I spot this street musician who I think might be John Lennon, but then I realize he's Jesus. Because it's a dream, I don't seem bothered by the fact that the Lord has become a busker. Eternity is a long time. Maybe he just felt like getting a job.

So I wait while Jesus finishes up his number, which is a sort of folksy blues song, and I ask him if he knows where I'm going. He points to the hat on the ground and I get the idea: no tip, no directions. So I fish through my pockets, and it is one of those awkward moments where I have twenty cents, which I know is too little, and a ten-dollar bill, which is a bit more than I want to spend for directions, even if the directions come from the Son of God. So I stand there for a while, because I know there is no way to ask for change. It's not like I can pick up the hat and keep the change that's in there and give him the ten. The streets are getting more crowded, and I realize I need to either move along or pony up. So finally (and with a bit of regret) I chuck the ten-dollar bill in the hat and wait for him to tell me where I need to go.

"The thing is, no matter where you go, there you are," Jesus says.

I wait a bit, but then it's clear that this is his idea of advice and this is all he's going to say. I'm annoyed because if I'd known he was going to give cheesy guru hippie advice, then I would have only kicked in the two dimes. So I turn to walk away and I hear the squeal of tires and I realize that I've walked straight into the road and a car is going to hit me. Then I wake up.

"I'm home!" my mom yelled out.

I realized the squeal that woke me up must have been the screech of the door when she came in. I sat up and tried to rub the sleep out of my eyes. My mouth felt funky, and it tasted as if I might have been chewing on Mr. Muffles's ears again. I scootched over to the end of the bed and tried to figure out what the whole thing meant. I always wanted to believe that if the Son of God appeared to me, he would have something useful to say. Or that it would be more impressive.

I stood up.

A religious vision.

That's it! I did a little dance and gave a whoop.

I didn't need to tell the truth about Darci and Kimberly. What I needed was for the truth to come out. Who did the telling wasn't important. In fact, it might be better if it wasn't me. People weren't going to believe me anyway without Colin backing me up. I needed a way for Darci or Kimberly to be the ones to tell the truth, and I had a perfect idea for how that might work. It was time for someone to have a religious vision.

30

God, I get the importance of honoring one's father and mother (although if you want me to honor my dad, you should have him come by once in a while) but I don't think it's asking too much for this to be a two-way street. As Aretha Franklin once said:

R-E-S-P-E-C-T
Find out what it means to me
R-E-S-P-E-C-T
Take care, TCB
Oh, sock it to me, sock it to me, sock it to me, sock it to me.

Now, I'm not so interested in the sock-it-to-me bit, but I wouldn't mind if once in a while my mom treated me like I wasn't a complete infant.

The idea was brilliant. I was starting to think the dream itself might have been divinely sent to give me the idea, because truly the plan was inspired. If I could get Darci or Kimberly to come clean, I didn't need to worry about any of the downsides of me being the one to tell. I just needed to convince them that their immortal souls were in peril. My best bet would be with Kimberly, as I wasn't sure Darci had a soul. How exactly I was going to do this was where the plan got a bit vague.

Implementing my plan might call for reinforcements, which would be difficult, as my reinforcement list was getting smaller all the time. It was also hard to plan the next step, because my mom was mad at me for not starting dinner.

There was a lot of heavy sighing and talk about how it wouldn't hurt me to pull my weight around the house. Considering that she's always talking about how she wants me to stay in Wheaton, you would think she could make me feel more welcome. However, I knew there was no point in arguing the case, particularly if I wanted her to let me participate in track. I needed to be at the meet this Saturday. It was regionals. I apologized for being an ingrate and began to bustle around making dinner. I suggested that she have a seat in the living room and that I would pull together some pasta. I didn't once mention that since she's the fan of Rachael Ray's *30-Minute Meals*, she would be the one better suited to this task.

My mom sat in the living room, watching me make

dinner. Whenever I caught her eyes, I would shoot over an adoring daughter smile. I filled a glass with crushed ice, a slice of lemon, and water and brought it over to her. I gave a small bow, more as a sign of respect than anything else, but it might have been going too far.

"What did you do?" my mom asked, giving me a sideways look. "Are you in trouble at school?"

"No. I just realized you were right, I should have made dinner."

"Uh-huh."

"I can be nice, you know."

"Oh, I know you can be nice. I'm just wondering what you're hoping to get from it."

"Thanks a lot, Mom. You make me sound like a really great person. I can be nice just for the sake of being nice, you know."

I could tell she didn't believe me. I went back to the kitchen and loaded up the plates with spaghetti. I delivered them to the table with a flourish.

"How are things at school?"

"I'm *not* in trouble."

"I've noticed Joann hasn't been around much."

"Yeah." I twirled the spaghetti around on my fork and tried to figure out how to explain it.

"One of those things where you're both mad and you're not even sure why you're mad anymore?"

I looked over at my mom, surprised.

"I wasn't born a mom. I went to high school myself." My mom put her fork down and pushed her chair away from the table. "Did I ever tell you why I left Wheaton?"

"No. I figured you wanted to do something different."

"Sort of. When I was in school, I had a crush on Thomas Evers."

"Reverend Evers?" My mouth curled up in disgust, and my mom burst out laughing.

"He wasn't a reverend then, he was just Thomas. He was two years ahead of me, and he was handsome and popular, and I think every girl in school had a thing for him."

"Did he do that nasty Donald Trump comb-over thing back then?"

"No. He used to keep his hair cut really short, sort of like a military buzz cut. He had this great body because he played every sport. He worked out all the time."

"Mom, I'm eating here. Could we please not talk about his body?"

"Fair enough. Take my word for it: Thomas was attractive. I thought about him all the time, mooned around, wishing he would notice me."

"Mooned?"

"Not dropping-pants moon, mooning meaning I liked him, but he didn't know I was alive. I used to write him these long poems where I would describe how much I loved him. Really bad romantic poems. They were a bit steamy." She blushed. "At any rate, Sheila Hunter found one of the poems. It must have fallen out of my notebook. We had math together."

"Sheila Hunter? Isn't that Mrs. Evers?"

"It is now."

"Oh my God. She gave him the poem, didn't she?"

"Worse. She read it out loud in the cafeteria."

"No!"

"Yes. I wanted to crawl under the table and disappear."

"What happened?"

"Not much really happened. I was a freshman and Thomas was a junior. He continued to pretend I wasn't alive. People teased me about it. They used to call me Lord Byron."

"I saw that nickname in your old yearbooks. I thought it was because English was your favorite subject."

"Nope. It came from my poetic ability." My mom made finger quotations around "poetic ability."

"That must have sucked."

"Thomas and Sheila started going out that year. When I look back at high school, I realize I spent most of my time hating being there. I couldn't wait to leave. I knew I wanted to live someplace where no one knew about the poem incident. I wanted a fresh start."

"I completely get that."

"But that's the thing. I thought if I moved away, I could move away from all of it, but the memories were still with me. The fact that I was shy and awkward didn't change just because I changed locations. I made the same mistakes, but in a new place with new people."

"No matter where you go, there you are," I said.

My mom looked over and broke into a smile. "That's right, pretty wise words. How did you get so smart?"

"Genetics," I said. "Apparently bitchy genes can also be passed down: Darci is just how you describe her mom."

"Apple doesn't fall far from the tree."

"You're doing that cliché thing again."

"Do you know why they don't send mules to college?" my mom asked.

"Nobody likes a smartass?" I said.

This joke has been knocking around our house for a long time. My mom raised her fork in acknowledgment and we shared a smile. I watched her eat. I tried to imagine what it would be like to have someone read your hot love poems out loud. I felt bad for my teenage mom. She looked up and noticed me watching her.

"I'm sorry things got so messed up," I said.

"Sometimes a wrong turn leads us to exactly where we need to be, not where we wanted to be. If I hadn't gone to Chicago, I wouldn't have met your dad."

"That might have been a good thing."

"But then I wouldn't have had you."

"And you wouldn't have had to drop out of college and move back here. You could have done anything you wanted."

My mom stood up suddenly and came over to my seat. She kneeled down so we were face-to-face. She took my chin in her hand and forced me to look her straight in the eyes.

"Never think for a minute that I regret having you. You are the thing I am most proud of in my life and the best thing that has ever happened to me. From the moment you were born, I knew my destiny was to love you with my whole heart. If I could do anything I wanted, anything in the whole world, then I would choose all over again to be your mom." She paused and looked at me, her face serious. "No matter what questions you have in life, the one thing you should never doubt is how much I love you."

My throat felt tight, and I could feel the tears in my eyes. I knew if I said anything, I was going to start crying and this would turn into one of those made-for-TV movie moments. My mom didn't break eye contact for a long time. Finally she leaned over and kissed my forehead and went back to her chair. We didn't say anything else for the rest of dinner. I stood up to clear the dishes, but she waved me off and started to collect everything off the table.

"I owe you an apology," she said.

"For what?"

"Sometimes parents want so badly to save our kids from getting hurt that we make a bad decision. I'll call Coach Attley and ask him to put you back on the team. You're a smart girl. You'll make the decisions that are right for you. I need to remember that they're your decisions to make now." She looked over her shoulder and gave me a smile as she left the room. I could hear her piling the dishes in the sink and the water running. I stood up and followed her into the kitchen.

"Mom?"

She turned off the water and faced me.

"I was being nice earlier with dinner and everything

because I was hoping to convince you to call Coach Attley. I wasn't doing it just to be nice."

"I figured you had your reasons."

"I'm sorry."

"Well then, we're both sorry, so let's call it even, okay?"

I stepped forward, and my mom and I hugged. It had been a long time since we'd had a good hug. I squeezed her tight.

"You're a good mom," I whispered into her hair.

"I've got my moments." She gave me an extra squeeze and let me go. "Why don't you go for a run? You're going to have to get yourself into shape if you want to be ready for the meet on Saturday."

"You sure?"

"Be home by eight." She looked at me. "And when I say eight, I mean eight, not eight fifteen or eight thirty. This touching mother-daughter moment doesn't mean I'm getting soft on curfew."

"I would never think of you as soft." I promised, holding my hand up as if I were taking a pledge. As I turned and headed out, my mom gave my butt a slap with her wet towel.

31

God, you used to show up all the time down here. Burning bushes, visions, pillar of clouds, personal messages to your chosen. Lately you seem to be keeping your appearances to things like showing up on the side of a grilled cheese sandwich. I'm all for a good melted cheese sandwich (especially if you make it with like a stick of butter and that otherwise nasty Kraft cheese that comes in the plastic wrapper), but I'm thinking you can do better than revealing your likeness on the side of toast. It's like Madonna choosing to play in a mall food court. Way beneath your level, is what I'm trying to say. Maybe like some bands, you don't want to be bothered with taking the show on the road anymore. Fair enough. So what I'm wondering is, would it bother you if I worked a little miracle magic on my own? Think of it as me being like one of those tribute bands—never as good as the original, but if you can't see the original, not half bad.

I didn't need to run very far before I realized who my potential reinforcement could be, even if it meant having to swallow my pride. I ran past Todd's house. The stroller mommy vigilantes were gone, but I was willing to bet the neighbors were watching the house like it was free cable. Spying on neighbors is an accepted activity in Wheaton. If I went up to the front door, it would take less than one minute for the news to spread through town, and that might mess with the plan. I ran down the street and then doubled back through the greenbelt so that I could approach the house from the back.

Victory. I could see Todd walk past one of the upper-story windows. I picked up a small stone and hurled it at the window. It plunked on the siding and fell back to the yard. It hardly made any sound at all. It's clear why running is my sport and not softball pitching. I picked up another stone and tried again. This one hit the ledge, but I still missed the window. I bent down, found another rock, and hurled it. I would have hit the window that time too, except for the fact that the window was now open and Todd was leaning out. I nailed him right between the eyes.

"Shit," Todd said, grabbing his head and then checking for blood. He winced and looked out. I gave a halfhearted wave.

"Proctor? Is that you?"

"Can you come down?"

He didn't say anything, but he shut the window and the light went off. I paced back and forth in the tree line while I waited. He came jogging out the back door. He was wearing a giant sweatshirt, and he pulled the hood up as he came out.

"You know, there is this brand-new technology you might have heard of called a doorbell. Or, if technology freaks you out, then you could try the traditional door-knocking thing."

"You okay?"

"You threw a rock at my head. I thought the towns-people had finally come to stone me."

"Sorry." I made patterns in the fallen pine needles with my shoes. "How have you been?"

"Do you mean how have I been since everyone thinks I've been trying to poison my classmates, or how've I been since I kissed you and you ran away without saying another word?"

"I meant more of just a general how have you been." I shuffled in place. "About when I was here last time. I left for a reason."

"Let me guess, it's complicated." Todd looked at me, then gave a sigh.

"You could have called me," I pointed out.

"Life's getting complicated here, too. My parents are talking about moving."

"Moving? Are you serious?"

"TES is a private school. They can kick me out with or without any proof. That means I either need to take my GED or transfer somewhere for the last couple months of school. Not to mention that everyone around here thinks I'm a psycho. I think my parents are afraid this could affect my self-image in a negative way. To be honest, I think their whole dream of living in America's heartland hasn't really panned out the way they thought. I think they want to go back to Chicago." He shot me a look. "I'm sort of surprised to see you."

"I wanted to talk to you, but I was grounded."

"Because you went out with me?"

"Sort of, more because my mom was doing this freak-out thing."

"Would she be mad that you're here now?"

"I don't think so, we've worked a few things out. I wanted to talk to you. I need your help with something."

Todd looked at me. I could tell he was trying to figure out what I was up to and if the whole thing was a joke.

"Okay."

I followed him into the back of the house, giving a quick look to see if any of his neighbors were watching. We walked through his kitchen; Mrs. Seaver was clearly a fan of the country look. I hadn't really looked around last time I was here. The house was stuffed with antiques, and the walls had old metal signs advertising oatmeal and coffee. The signs were dinged up and faded, but cool. I paused to look them over. The room smelled like caramelized sugar and chocolate. Someone must have been baking. My nose twitched like a rabbit.

Todd walked into the living room, flopped into a big leather club chair, and motioned to the sofa. I sat down and sank into the piles of pillows. It was possible I would need a crane to get out of there. I noticed that Todd hadn't chosen to sit next to me, which gave me the feeling he wasn't quite over the whole walkout incident.

"So what's up?" Todd asked.

"I wanted to know if you could help me with something."

"Depends."

"Okay, here's the thing. I need you to promise not to tell anyone what I'm about to tell you."

"Can't do that."

I shut my mouth with a click. I hadn't been expecting that answer.

"Why not? You don't trust me?"

"Nope. I've got no reason to trust you," said Todd, without breaking eye contact. "It isn't that I don't want to."

"But you don't."

"Nothing personal, but I'm not real trusting lately."

Todd's reaction was less than ideal. I wasn't thinking that he was going to be my knight in shining armor, but I had been hoping that he would just fall for my feminine wiles without thinking about things too much. So much for wiles.

"Then I don't know if I can talk to you," I countered in what I hoped was an enticing manner.

Todd stood up and brushed his pants off.

"Well, thanks for stopping by."

"Are you serious?"

"Completely."

I sat there twisting the fringe on one of the pillows while I thought over my options.

"Okay, you don't have to promise."

Todd flopped back down in the chair and motioned for me to start talking.

"I know that Darci and Kimberly are lying about what happened. There was never anyone after them. No one slipped them anything. They took something out at the

Barn, some pills, and that's why Kimberly got sick."

"What about everyone else who got sick?"

"I have no idea what happened with everyone else. I'm pretty sure Darci took the same stuff later to make it look good when she had her fit. Or she faked the whole thing. I'm guessing the rest of them are faking it to fit in."

Todd paused, thinking it over.

"I guess it could be psychosomatic."

"Huh?"

"In their heads. It can happen with groups. It's like groupthink. If you tell someone you smell something, you can convince a whole crowd of people they smell it too. There have been case studies where schools have been evacuated because everyone was sure there was some gas or something, kids getting sick, throwing up, you name it, only there really wasn't anything there. It's group panic. You believe it and then your body responds."

"Well, there you go. It's psychosomatic."

"How do you know Kimberly took pills?"

"First, I don't know how well you know Kimberly, but there isn't anything she wouldn't try in pursuit of a party. There was this one party out at the Barn last year, and everyone brought whatever booze they had stolen from their folks. So there was this toxic mixture of orange juice, vodka, rum, beer, coolers, and then some guy brought a bottle of Bailey's Irish Cream. So when the Bailey's met the rest of that mixture, it formed these, like, clots on the surface. Like booze dumplings."

"That's disgusting."

"Exactly. You're not even seeing it, let alone smelling it. It was nasty. Everyone at the party was ticked because now the stuff was undrinkable, but Kimberly fished those Bailey's clots out of the mixture and *ate* them. That's the kind of girl she is."

"Nice. Still doesn't prove anything."

"I'm telling you I know for a fact that she and Darci made up their story. They weren't home that night, they were at a party out at the Barn. I was there and I saw them. I left before they saw me."

"So if you know, why haven't you said anything before now?"

"It's complicated, but I couldn't. I still can't."

"So you came over here to tell me you know that I'm being blamed for something I didn't do, but that because it's 'complicated' you can't actually help me?"

"But I *can* help you. I've got a plan."

"Okay," he said slowly.

I leaned forward to tell him my plan.

“We give Kimberly a religious vision and tell her that God wants her to confess. I’m thinking it should be Kimberly, because it’s possible Darci doesn’t have a soul. Kimberly is way more naïve, too. We have God tell her that if she doesn’t come clean before the show this weekend, her immortal soul is in peril. Real fire-and-brimstone kind of stuff.”

“A vision.”

Todd didn’t sound convinced. I had hoped he would recognize a good plan when he saw one. I’m not saying I expected him to fall to his knees in gratitude, but I expected a bit more of a positive reaction. Then again, it’s possible religious visions aren’t big in the Jewish faith, and therefore he was underestimating the power.

“Yep. I’ve been thinking, and I’ve got a pretty good idea. If we went to the Barn and set up like a gas fireplace fixture thingy, then we could make some kind of burning bush effect. Basically, we need a fire that doesn’t burn out. We would have to hide the mechanics, but there has to be a way to do that. You’re really good in the sciences, so maybe you could handle that part. As long as she doesn’t look too close, it will work. If she thinks it’s God in there, I’m thinking she won’t investigate. We’ll have to go into Fort Wayne and go to a Home Depot to get the stuff. They would have everything we need to make it work, and no one knows us there. We set it up and then we trick her out there somehow. We hide up in the hayloft and play a tape recording of our voices, so that we can disguise them somehow, telling her to tell the truth or risk burning in hell."

"Are you serious?"

"Well, if you can think of something else, I'm open. The thing is, we have to make sure she doesn't recognize us, and it has to be appropriately miracle-like."

Todd didn't say anything for a moment. Then he leaned forward quickly.

"I know! We could do some kind of parting of the Red Sea thing, only instead of the Red Sea it would have to be the pond on the Emerson lot. Maybe with some of those pumps from the hardware store."

"Do you think it would work?"

Todd burst out with a harsh laugh.

"No, it wouldn't work. Neither will your burning bush plan. You start a fire of any sort in the Barn, and between the old wood and the garbage lying around, that place would go up in record time. Then, in addition to the trouble I'm in, I could add arson. Great plan. Thanks for coming over. Maybe later you could get me involved in some other felony."

"I'm not saying the plan doesn't need work." I felt a bit annoyed. "It's easier to criticize other people's ideas than to come up with your own."

"I have a plan. How about you go to the school and tell them your big secret? Tell them how you know the whole thing is a lie."

"I can't do that," I said. "No one would believe me."

"How do you know unless you try?"

"It wouldn't work. I tried telling my own mom and she didn't believe me. I can't."

"Can't or won't?"

"I'm telling you, it's complicated."

"Life's complicated, Proctor." Todd stood, putting an end to our meeting. "You know, I actually thought for a minute that maybe you came out here because you liked me."

"I do like you."

"No, you like the idea of liking somebody different. You don't care about me at all."

"I can't explain, but you have to trust me. This isn't easy for me."

"If you want it to be easy, then you're going to be pretty fucking disappointed. If you can't handle the complications in a small town, there's no way you can handle someplace like Chicago."

I stood up in a huff, or to be more honest I swam around in the pillows for a few seconds while I tried to heave myself out of the quicksand couch. I pointed a finger at him. "Don't be so sanctimonious."

"Oooh, fancy SAT word."

"Don't be an ass. If you think it's easier in a small town, then you're wrong."

"It's not easy in a big city, either, just easier to hide from shit you don't want to face."

I opened my mouth to say something really foul, when Todd's mom walked into the room. She was tiny. I've seen fourth graders who were taller than Mrs. Seaver. She had dark, curly hair and small features. It looked like she was half human and half elf. I choked on the words that were about to fly out of my mouth.

"Hello! I'm Mrs. Seaver." She gave me a warm smile. "Did Todd offer you anything to drink? He didn't tell me he was having any friends over."

"Emma just stopped by. She can't stay," said Todd.

"That's no reason not to be a decent host. Boys," she said, looking at me with a shake of her head. "Can I offer you anything? We've got juice and some soda." She gestured toward the kitchen.

"No thank you, ma'am."

"Emma has to be going. She's got all these complicated things on her plate," Todd said.

I felt my lip twitch, but I didn't say anything. I just kept smiling.

"Well, I'll get out of your hair." His mom gave my arm a pat as she walked out of the room.

Todd and I both waited for her to leave and then faced off.

"There is no reason for you to be an ass," I hissed at him.

"There is no reason for me to be nice, either," he said. "This has nothing to do with me. You think you're so different from everyone here, but you're not. You're just like them. Make it look it good, but don't worry about the truth. You can let yourself out."

I chucked the throw pillow at his back, but if I was hoping for an impressive gesture I should have thrown something harder than a down pillow. It nearly fluttered to the floor, it was so light. Todd turned around and raised an eyebrow and then walked out. I took a couple of deep breaths and then headed back through the kitchen.

Mrs. Seaver was taking cookies out of the oven. "Are you sure you have to leave?"

"Yes, ma'am. I was out for a run and just stopped by. I've got a curfew."

"All these ma'ams make me feel old. You just call me Carol."

I wasn't sure what to say. Wheaton is one of those towns where calling an adult anything other than Mr., Mrs., sir, or ma'am is a near-criminal offense. I was no more likely to call her Carol than I was to sprout wings and fly home. I settled for a vague smile.

"Do you want a cookie?" She held out two cookies on a napkin. I reached out and took them. They were still warm. I ate one of the cookies in two bites.

"Thanks. I have to go." I gestured toward the door.

She waved, and I moved to the sliding door that led to their backyard.

"I'm glad you came over. Things have been hard on Todd. It's good to know he has some friends he can count on."

I felt the cookie I just ate start to claw its way back up, and I gave a big swallow to push it back down.

"Yeah, well." I couldn't think of anything to add, so I raised the other cookie in a salute, and headed out. I tried not to look around when I left. I figured Mrs. Seaver didn't deserve to know I was embarrassed to be seen at her house.

I walked about a block and then threw the other cookie into the woods. It tasted great, but for some reason the idea of trying to eat it made me feel like I would throw up.

Mrs. Seaver was really nice. I hoped she wouldn't find the cookie I tossed and think that I didn't like her baking.

No one could say that I hadn't tried. I looked up in the sky.

"God?" I paused, in case he wanted to respond. Nothing except for the chirp of the birds. "God. I need a sign here. It doesn't have to be a burning bush or anything, but a small sign. Maybe a crack of lightning or something."

I sat down and waited. No lightning.

"Okay, God? How about if you want me to do something, you have a squirrel run by right now." I looked around. Nothing. "Okay, then how about right now?" I waited again. Not a single squirrel. This is saying something. Wheaton has a significant squirrel population.

I got up and started running home. Whatever happened next wasn't going to be my problem. If God couldn't be bothered, why should I?

Coach Attley was the only one who didn't seem to care about Reverend Teaks. He was completely focused on the big regional track meet on Saturday. He hadn't had a kid get a track scholarship in his entire coaching career. If I got a scholarship offer from Northwestern, this would be his gold-medal moment. He scheduled extra practices for me and would find me in the hallways to pass me his latest strategy. He had been Googling nutrition sites and was coming up with all these food concoctions that he wanted me to eat. We had a debate about the pros and cons of drinking a raw egg shake on the morning of the meet. Coach Attley felt strongly that the rush of protein would give me energy. I countered with my view that projectile vomiting would certainly be an issue to forward motion.

On Friday I was sitting in the cafeteria (with my pariah circle of empty chairs around me), waiting for Coach Attley to meet me. He wanted to give me some kind of protein bar that he was certain was going to do the trick. I was so out of it that I didn't even know they were planning to announce the top three nominees for the king and queen court for the dance until Mr. Karp's voice broke out over the PA system.

"If I could get everyone's attention!"

The room turned to face the PA box wedged in a ceiling corner.

32

God, you'll have to excuse me if I don't have much to say. To be honest, I'm getting a bit tired of our one-way conversations. I guess it's a case of if you don't have anything good to say, you shouldn't say anything at all, and I guess neither of us has anything good to say.

If I didn't suck at math so much, I most likely could have figured out the exact number of days, hours, and seconds before graduation. Of course, I still could always learn math. I had the time, because pretty much no one was talking to me.

Joann was too busy hanging out with Darci and her crew. I tried to talk to her about it, but she kept insisting there wasn't a problem, she just needed to help with the dance. She didn't invite me to help or sit at the table with the others anymore, and I didn't ask. I ate my lunch in the library. Awkward conversations with Colin weren't a problem, because he didn't talk to me at all. Todd still wasn't coming to school, and I noticed he wasn't beating a path to my door to apologize, either. Everyone else in school was certain that I was a Jesus-hating freak, thanks to the fight with Joann. New SAT word: ostracized.

The news about Joann and Colin becoming "promised" (whatever the hell that meant) was becoming a story larger than the TES terrorist. Turns out romance trumps terror. Girls vaulted over one another to get a look at the ring on Joann's finger. She kept the ring polished to a blinding shine and developed this way of talking where she waved her hands all around like she was constantly in the process of directing an orchestra. Joann and Colin were the first couple in our class to "declare their intentions," and everyone thought it was the cutest thing ever. Joann was already talking about wedding colors and flowers, all for a wedding that was still years away in theory. Because I was following a new approach of staying out of things, I didn't once bring up the fact that people who marry young tend to divorce at a higher rate. Plus, I hear they gain weight and start wearing those high-waisted mom jeans at a frighteningly high percentage. I also kept those thoughts to myself.

I was the leper of TES. Jesus might have preached that we should be nice to the lepers, but there weren't any budding Mother Teresa types around here. Everyone avoided me as if I were leaving a trail of rotted fingers and toes in my wake. There are several advantages to being a social pariah:

- You have a chance to get a lot of homework done when there is no distraction by any form of social interaction.
- You aren't forced to listen to people do a neckline-to-hem breakdown of what dress they're planning to wear to the spring dance and be forced to act as if you care.
- You don't have to worry about anyone catching you rolling your eyes when they talk about how great it is that Reverend Teaks is coming to town.
- No one pressures you for part of your lunch, to borrow your favorite pen, or for the answers to the biology homework.
- You can focus on the upcoming track meet and practice the sports visualization techniques Coach Attley keeps talking ab

"I would like to announce the royal court for this year's spring dance, Undersea Adventure."

There was a murmur of voices in the cafeteria and a couple of girly squeals. I saw Darci reach up and pat her hair into place and do a quick swipe of her mouth with her finger. Nothing worse than accepting your scepter with tuna salad caught in your teeth.

"I am quite certain that this year's king and queen and the court will be a testament to our school. It has been a difficult few months for everyone, and I know all of us are looking forward to the celebration of our faith with Reverend Teaks tomorrow and the dance after that."

Another round of girlish squeals. Kimberly was basically crawling up Darci's side with excitement.

"Please join me in welcoming this year's royal court."

Darci sat straight up, her hand slightly extended ready to take the arm of her boyfriend Justin or perhaps so the rest of us could kiss it.

"Kimberly Ryan and Richard Naslund."

Kimberly flushed bright red and covered her face. Richard pumped his arm in the air as if he had won a major sporting event. Darci shot Kimberly a smile before turning back to face the speaker.

"Darci Evers and Justin Miller."

Darci stood up, but before she could take center stage, Mr. Karp announced the third couple.

"Joann Delaney and Colin Stewart."

There was a beat of silence where no one said anything. And then Joann let out a squeak. The girls surrounded her, jumping up and down. Colin shuffled over from the jock table and reached in to grab Joann. He held her hand. Joann was doing the full-on Miss America moment. She was crying, and one hand was over her heart. The crowd yelled for them to kiss, and Colin leaned in and gave Joann a peck on the cheek. The cafeteria erupted with cheers. I suspected Joann's recent ring had tipped the scale in her favor, although it was clear she never expected it. Joann was happier than I had ever seen her. I smiled. She deserved this. Based on everyone's reaction, she and Colin were a shoo-in for the king and queen.

The smile fell off my face. There was clearly one person who was not sharing in the joy of this moment. Darci stood to the left of the group. Justin reached her side, and she swatted away his hand. Her mouth was turned into a snarl and her eyes were glacial cold. I could see that she was breathing heavily, and if she had been a dragon I would have fully expected flames to shoot out of her nose.

"Oh my gosh! I just can't believe it!" Joann reached over to include Darci in the group hug.

The snarl on Darci's face morphed into a smile. The kind of smile that you see on psychos in horror movies.

"I'm so happy for you," Darci cooed. "It will be so much fun for all of us to be on the court together." Darci leaned in and hugged Joann. The crowd oohed and aahed. I could tell that everyone believed Darci, but I could still see her face. She might have been hugging Joann, but I could tell she was looking for a place to stick the knife.

33

God, I know lately we haven't been on speaking terms, but please, please let me run well. It matters. It matters so much.

It was possible that Coach Attley was more keyed up than I was. He drummed his fingers on the steering wheel in a nervous riff and kept changing the radio stations. I couldn't watch him. It just made me, if possible, even more anxious. I stared out the van window as we drove out of town. The rest of my teammates were equally quiet. It was early; the sun was creeping over the giant white tent set up in the Hansens' field. It looked like the circus had come to town, only instead of a ringmaster, we would have the Reverend Teaks. A few news vans had arrived sometime in the night, and I suspected there would be more when the show went live. People were scurrying around and unloading folding chairs from a truck. There was a large satellite dish on top of a truck, turned toward the sky like a flower. I looked away.

The track meet was being held in Fort Wayne. When we got there the track was wet. It must have rained the night before. The rain would make it slick, harder to get purchase, less than ideal. I walked in slow circles as if I were lost. I felt like I needed to get my bearings. A group from another school was spread out on mats, doing their stretches. The meet pulled in ten different schools. There was going to be some serious competition. I did a few stretches and kept walking.

The stands were starting to fill. A few of the schools seemed to have brought full sections of color-coordinated cheering squads. They waved hand-painted signs whenever someone from their school wandered past. There wouldn't be many people from Wheaton. The Spirit Squad! spent their hard-earned cheering abilities only on sports that mattered.

I searched the crowd to see if I could spot the scouts. I figured it would be asking too much for them to be wearing the distinctive purple Northwestern colors with a giant SCOUT painted on their jackets. I walked back to our team's bench, swinging my arms to get the blood moving. The voice on the PA announced that they would be starting with the long jump in just a few minutes. A few kids started moving in that direction.

"GO PROCTOR!" a voice yelled out.

I spun around and searched the crowd. My mom stood up and gave another whoop. I didn't know she had been planning to come. She had a giant foam WE'RE NUMBER ONE finger on her hand. I had no idea where she got it. Are there stores that sell nothing but foam fingers? She waved the finger wildly, and I found myself breaking into a smile. I gave her a wild wave back.

It was going to be okay.

My first race was hurdles. Coach Attley was on the sidelines screaming last-minute advice, which I couldn't even hear. I put my feet in the blocks and did my best to clear my mind. When the starter pistol rang out, I felt myself take off in a fluid motion. I was up and over the first hurdle. I could feel my arms and legs pumping, synchronized, my legs stretching out perfectly. I didn't dare risk a look around to see where everyone else was at, but I could tell no one was in front of me. I heard a bang as someone knocked over a hurdle, the clang of the metal as it hit the track. Someone was out of it.

I was up and almost over the last hurdle when it happened. The tip of my toe caught the crossbar and I fell to the ground, my hands sliding on the gravel. I saw someone pass me on the left. I pushed up and was on my feet in less than a second. Another racer passed me as I tried to find my rhythm again. My breath was ragged, but I pushed forward, staring at the back of the person directly in front of me. I stretched forward at the line, barely beating that racer, but I could see that someone else had already won. Shit. I slowed to a walk, my hands on my hips. They stung, and when I looked down I saw they were bleeding. Great.

"You okay?" Coach Attley was at my side in a second.

"I lost," I wheezed.

"You came in second."

"Second doesn't impress scouts. No one offers the runner-up a scholarship. Second is losing."

"Second is second. You don't know what the scouts think. Let me see your hands."

I held my palms up. Coach Attley poured some water from his water bottle over them and I gave a hiss. He patted at the palms with a towel he was holding.

"Your hands are okay. We should get some Neosporin on them. None of the cuts look deep, mostly scratches. You twist anything? You popped up pretty quick."

"I was sure I could still win it." I felt tears gather in my eyes. I didn't know how to explain it, but I had been so sure that I would win. Everything was based on winning. Winning this race, winning the scholarship, winning a way out of here. I didn't even have a freaking plan B. I wouldn't say that I believed in destiny, but I believed in planning. Everything I had been working toward was based on the plan that I would win. I hadn't allowed myself to think I could lose. I didn't want to cry. Coach Attley was not a big fan of tears. He gave me a whack on the back that nearly threw me back down to my knees.

"You need to put this race behind you. You've got the hundred meters in about ten minutes, so keep walking around, make sure you don't stiffen up. Get some water into you too. I want you hydrated."

"Hurdles are always my best race." I didn't say the rest, but I was thinking it. If I couldn't win in hurdles, what were my odds in the other events?

"You mean, hurdles have always been your best. You've got another race in ten minutes. Today you might discover the hundred meters is your best. No looking back." Coach Attley looked around. "Okay, I've got to go check on Simpson. She's up next on pole vault. Pull yourself together. I'll be right back." Coach Attley gave me another whack and jogged off. Any more of these reassuring whacks and I was going to end up bruised.

As I walked along the inner ring, I tried to figure out what went wrong. I never snag on the hurdles. Never. Up ahead I saw the girl who came in first. Her teammates were giving her high fives. Her hair was braided, with small white beads on the ends. They clicked and swayed together. I waited until her teammates left and walked over.

"Good race," I said.

"You too," she said with a smile.

"Right until I wiped out." I held out my bloody hands.

"Doesn't matter that you fell, it matters that you got up."

She gave me a smile and jogged off. I stood watching her for a second. I looked up in the stands, and my mom gave me a thumbs-up. Track wasn't her sport. It's possible she thought you were supposed to fall over. I shot her a thumbs-up back and made my way over to the other track while I drank water and tried to forget what had happened and the fact that the community college most likely didn't even have a track team.

The hundred meters is always a big event, and at a regional meet like this, the best runners always turn out for it. I wasn't surprised to see the girl who beat me in hurdles a few lanes over. We gave each other a nod as we lined up. My brain was racing, but when the pistol went off it was instantly blank. My vision narrowed, and I didn't so much run as I flew to the finish line. When I crossed the line, I knew I'd won it.

The first voice I heard clearly was my mom's, the second was Attley's, and then the rest of my team. I stopped and the team surrounded me.

"Looks like the hundred meters is your race after all, Proctor," Attley said, giving me another one of his back-snapping whacks. "There are some people who want to meet you."

Attley clamped his hand on my shoulder and led me over to the sidelines. A man and a woman stood there. He was holding a clipboard. They had to be the scouts. I rubbed my nose quickly and tried to stand straighter.

"Congratulations on the win," the woman said.

"Emma, these folks are from Northwestern."

"Go Wildcats!" I said, and they both smiled.

"We understand you're interested in our track program?"

"Yes, ma'am."

"We heard from admissions that you've been accepted to the university. Have you made a decision yet about whether you'll be joining us?"

"I'd love to, but it's going to come down to finances."

"Well, you keep running like this and maybe we can help you out with some of that."

I felt my mouth split into a huge smile. Was this it? Would they tell me if I had a full ride right now?

"She's my best," Attley said, standing proudly next to me. "She's got the drive and focus. I think you folks would be real lucky to get her."

"We'll be sending out scholarship letters in the next couple of weeks, along with the financial aid packages. We keep seeing times likes these in your next couple of meets and I think we'll send you a letter that means you'll be wearing purple next year."

I managed to wait until they walked away, but then I gave a yell. Attley even hugged me, which never happens. I searched the crowd and found my mom. I gave Attley a pleading look. We weren't allowed to leave the track oval during meets. Coach Attley was a big believer in either sticking together as a team or sitting in the stands with your friends. He didn't think people should do both.

"Aw, go on, go tell her," Attley said, still grinning something fierce.

My mom met me in the stairwell leading into the bleachers. She looked like she might cry. She held up the letter from Northwestern that I had left on the kitchen table that morning.

"Look at you," she said, giving me a hug. "You worked

for this and you've earned it. I'm so proud of you, Emma."

I held on to her and tried not to think about Todd or the rest of them. It was a clear-cut, every-man-for-himself kind of situation. I *had* worked for this. I earned it on my own. I'd tried to tell my mom about the Barn and she hadn't believed me, I'd tried to convince Colin and he didn't want to be involved, everyone was blaming everyone else, Joann wasn't even really my friend anymore, and Todd wasn't willing to fix the problem any way except his way. I had done the best I could. I didn't owe anyone anything. Wishing everything could have worked out would be like wishing Tinkerbell would come and take you away from all your problems. A nice idea, but not reality. Still, I'd thought winning would feel better than it did.

It seems some prayers are answered, but you don't get to choose which ones.

34

God, I'm thinking you might be more popular if some of the people who spoke for you weren't so, well, annoying. On the other hand, at least you have people who want to be your friends, which is more than I can say for myself.

I considered skipping Reverend Teaks's amazing Faith Forward road show, but it felt like a required activity in some way, or maybe more like a dare. Either way, I was going. I did indulge in several fantasies on how I wanted the show to go, however.

- Reverend Teaks would lay his hands on someone in the crowd to heal them and they would keel over with a heart attack instead.
- Reverend Teaks would swear to be saying what God wanted, or may God strike him

dead, and then a bolt of lightning would shoot out of the sky and take him out.

- A convenient plague of locusts would swarm over the tent (or frogs, or any other icky creepy-crawly creature) and cover it completely.
- Through some freak technical difficulty, the live feed would cross with the porn channel and pump that into millions of American homes instead.
- *60 Minutes* or *Dateline* would show up with an exposé proving that Reverend Teaks was some kind of secret sexual pervert who molested dogs or maybe cross-dressing dwarves.

Outside the tent, people were milling about, and the scene had the feel of a rock concert. The TV crews were set up on the side, and reporters were interviewing people from the town. I could see the owner of Sheer Beauty doing her best to comment on the rise of teen violence, which was impressive after her years of inhaling perm solution, which had made stringing sentences together a challenge for her. A few of the kids from school were pushing and shoving to have their moment on camera and share how they survived the horror. I slipped past all of them and went in. The tent was almost full. It looked like a few people had come first thing that morning to nab the seats right at the front. The audience was mostly in rows of folding chairs, but in the very back were a few rows of bleachers. I slipped into a back row, scooting past a few people to take a seat on the aluminum bench.

If you looked at the stage, you would never imagine it was in a field in Middle of Nowhere, Indiana. The stage platform was covered in a dark blue carpet, and behind it were yards of drapes in a lighter, shimmery blue. On the side they had cordoned off an area for the choir, and across from them were the cameras. The choir was jostling for position, and I immediately spotted Darci. She had gone all out for the occasion. She had done her hair in a style that might best be described as "huge." Her hair had to be as tall as a toddler. She must have backcombed and used a case of hair spray.

A few of the girls from school, including Joann, walked up to the choir to wish them luck. Joann looked nice. I could tell she'd curled her hair. She was wearing a corsage, just like Darci and Kimberly, the only acknowledgment of their special status as spring dance royalty. I thought of trying to flag her down, but before I could even raise my hand all the way, I tucked it back in my lap. She wasn't going to sit with me. I fingered the track medal I had brought with me, flipping it back and forth in my hand. I had my win, and Joann was going to have hers. She deserved to be royalty; it suited her. I was sure that tonight she'd be crowned queen, too. It didn't matter if I thought the whole thing was stupid, what mattered was that she was my friend and it was important to her. I saw Darci start gesturing madly as if a crisis were at hand, and Joann reached for her purse. Whatever Darci needed, Joann would have it. Safety pins, asprin, Band-Aids, small snacks, possibly an outline from the UN on how to negotiate peace. Joann is that kind of person, always prepared. Darci took the purse from her, fished around in it, and pulled out a tube of lip gloss. When she handed back the purse, she made such a big deal out of it you would think Joann had lent her a kidney instead of a lip balm.

Suddenly the organ music started, and everyone hustled to get to their seats. A bank of hot lights behind us clicked on for the cameras. I could feel them giving off heat already. I was going to end up with a tan by the time the show was over.

Reverends Evers and Teaks came out on the stage, and the crowd burst into applause that nearly drowned out the organ. Reverend Teaks motioned for quiet, while keeping his best side to the camera. Behind the cameras was a fellow wearing a headset and holding up a giant sign that said APPLAUSE.

"Now, now, no need to glorify me, we come here today to glorify God!" Teaks roared out.

It was hard to tell if it was his inspirational words or the fact that the guy holding the applause sign was now basically jumping up and down in the universal sign language for "kick it up a notch," but the crowd roared its approval. Teaks held his arms open wide as if he was bathing in the adulation. He looked a bit orange, and there was a thin line under his chin where the makeup hadn't been blended in. Reverend Evers looked pale and pasty next to him. I suspected that on TV, Teaks would look great and Evers would end up looking like Voldemort's pasty younger brother.

"We come to you today live from Wheaton, Indiana. The heartland of America. And it *is* the heartland. As I've been among these people I have felt the beat, beat, beat, beating of their hearts, but instead of pumping blood, what they pump is faith. This town is doing its best to spread the faith they have to our entire nation. We came here because we can learn from the good folks in Wheaton. This isn't a town that worships Hollywood or rock stars. No, sir, this is a town that worships the only one true God. They are soldiers in God's army. They are not afraid to stand and fight for him. No, this is a town that puts its faith front and center. They put their Faith Forward!"

The crowd gave another cheer, and the producer gave a signal and the choir broke into their first song. They apparently were trying out some choreography. They sort of swayed right two beats, then left, then a quick clap in the center. It wasn't exactly a move that was going to catapult anyone to the top of *So You Think You Can Dance*. Despite this, one of the choir members was having trouble. She went right when everyone else was going left. At one point she bumped into Darci, who nearly pushed her to the ground. I had the feeling that anyone who got in the way of Darci's camera angle today was going to pay big-time.

"I'm about to tell you a story, but it's not a Bible story. It's not a bedtime story. No! This story may scare some; it's a story of how Satan can find his way anywhere. He slinks in on the TV and in the records. He hides behind the idea of being politically correct. He whispers in our ears that maybe some things are okay. That it's okay to have sex outside of marriage, that maybe it is okay to challenge what it means to be a family. He sneaks into the hearts of those who are too weak to fight him. And what gives people strength?"

The producer held up another sign off camera. This one said JESUS in giant black letters.

"JESUS!" the crowd yelled out. Say what you will about Wheaton, we sure could read.

"That's right! Jesus gives people strength, but there were people in this town who didn't worship our Lord. Oh no. They were not part of the heartland, for their hearts were black. A nation relies on its children as the future, and there were those here who wanted to cut down our future. Can we stand for this?"

The producer held up another sign, this one with the word NO. I think he really needed to give us a bit more credit. We could have worked that one out without the flash card.

"We live in dark times. Times when our children threaten one another. When even our schools are not safe, not safe from the inside. Here in Wheaton there were those who would harm their fellow students, who planned to bring down their school, and do you know what saved them? Was it luck?"

"No!" the crowd shouted out, due in part, no doubt, to the helpful signage.

"Was it the law that saved them?"

"No!"

"Was it coincidence?"

"No!"

"Was it logic or fancy *CSI* kinds of science?"

"No!"

"That's right. It was faith. It was faith that kept our children safe. It was faith that ferreted out the sinners. It was faith that purged this community clean and it will be faith that will take this community forward!"

I glanced around the tent. Joann and Colin were sitting together and if I had to guess, they were holding hands, but I couldn't tell from here. Both of their families were there too, sitting just a few rows back. It seemed like almost all of Wheaton was in the tent. None of the kids who had been blamed were here, or their families, which was probably for the best. It looked like the crowd could rile themselves up into a proper witch burning. Anything to keep things pure. I shifted in my seat. I wasn't sure how any of the accused were going to be able to come back to TES or even deal with living here. Normally I would consider being banned from Wheaton a good thing, but I knew some of them would want to stay.

Teaks had loosened his tie, and the sweat was starting to stream down his face. Of course, with the bright lights directly behind me, I was doing some sweating of my own. I felt nauseated. Between the heat, the loud, booming voice of Teaks, and everyone cheering, I was rethinking the wisdom of coming. I looked down the aisle and tried to figure if there would be a way to sneak out. I didn't belong and didn't even feel like trying to pretend I did anymore.

The choir finished another song, and Reverend Teaks walked over to them. Darci stood up straighter. She could tell the cameras were on her. However, Teaks was headed for Kimberly. He placed a hand on her shoulder. Kimberly looked like she was ready to pass out again. It was like she had been pulled out of a crowd by a rock star at a concert.

"We're going to pray over this girl. This girl was the first to be struck. She hovered near death. Do you think the doctors knew what to do? No, they did not. They were ready to throw their hands up, but you know what? The rest of the town threw their hands up! They didn't throw them up in surrender, they threw them up in prayer, and their prayers were answered."

A few people yelled out amens. I stood up. I was done.

I started to excuse myself and shuffle out of the row. That's when I heard Darci's voice.

"Reverend!"

I turned around in the aisle. Darci had fallen on her knees in front of Teaks. He looked over, surprised; this apparently had not gone down in dress rehearsal.

"Reverend, I've sinned and Jesus wants me to repent!"

I had no doubt Darci had a lot of repenting to do and plenty of sins that could be catalogued, but I doubted her motives.

"I haven't been honest, Reverend. I allowed friendship to slip between me and the Lord. Between me and the truth. We aren't safe yet. There's still another involved in the plan. I didn't want to turn her in, because she's a friend. Now I realize, Reverend Teaks, it isn't for me to protect her, it's up to the Lord to judge her motives." Darci looked out over the crowd, her arm outstretched with a pointing finger. She smiled, her lips turning up slightly. Suddenly I knew exactly where her finger would stop.

Darci pointed directly at Joann. Everyone followed Darci's finger and stared at my best friend. The people next to her took a step back. Joann's head spun as she looked around in confusion.

"I . . . I wouldn't hurt anyone," Joann stammered.

"She was a part of the group that was planning to hurt kids," Darci said.

I could see the shock in Joann's eyes. She couldn't figure out what was going on, but I could. They didn't make a school poisoner the queen of the spring dance. Darci was in the middle of a royal assignation, and Joann still didn't see it coming.

"I had nothing to do with it!"

"Do you swear? Here before God?" Reverend Teaks bellowed. He wasn't going to let Darci steal his show; if there was some witch burning to be done, he was going to be the one lighting the kindling.

Joann nodded madly. I willed her to shut her mouth and just walk away, but she looked pinned down. She was so sure the fact that she was telling the truth would be enough. "I was never involved, I swear!"

Reverend Teaks looked at a complete loss. There was no script for this turn of events, and the focus wasn't on him—two things he was poorly prepared to handle.

"Check her purse," Darci said.

Joann clutched her purse, pulling it closer. "No."

"What are you hiding?" someone in the back yelled out.

"Give me the purse, young lady. If you are right with

the Lord, you have nothing to fear," said Reverend Teaks, his arm held out.

Joann held it out, and even from here I could see her hand shaking.

Reverend Teaks reached into the bag and fished around. Suddenly he stopped and looked at her. He pulled his hand out, his fist tight. He opened it slowly, everyone leaning forward. A camera zoomed in on his hand, filling the screen behind his head.

There in his palm was a bottle. The camera zoomed in enough that you could see the label on the side: trinity evangelical secondary chemistry lab.

Joann's eyes widened. He might as well have pulled a rabbit out of her purse. Teaks held up the evidence and turned slowly in a circle so everyone could see.

"On your knees!" Teaks roared when he completed the circle, and Joann took a step back. She shook her head. "Repent!"

"I didn't—"

"Repent," the crowd called out. This time they didn't need any signs.

Darci stood to the side with a small smile. Joann looked ready to cry. A few people in the crowd were looking around uncertainly. I held my breath, waiting for someone to jump to Joann's defense. It was one thing for Darci to pick on those on the outside, but Joann had friends. Someone would stick up for her. My hand rubbed the front of the track medal as if I were trying to wear the letters down.

Joann's face was pale, and her eyes were full of tears. Then it occurred to me: You either waited for someone else to do the right thing, or you stood up and did it yourself. Winning wasn't about medals, it was about choices. I was scared, but I was more scared that I would be the kind of person who sat back and waited. Maybe the only way you become the kind of person you want to be is by acting like it.

"Stop," I yelled. Reverend Teaks couldn't hear my voice over the crowd, but the people near me turned around. I pushed toward the front. "Stop it."

I stopped and looked around. Everyone was facing me.

"I have a confession to make," I said. I took a deep breath, my hand tightly clutching the track medal in my pocket as if it were a lucky charm. "I've lied about what I knew too. I lied because it made things easier for me, and for that I'm ashamed." I turned to face Darci. "Joann didn't have anything to do with all this, and you know it. Neither did Stu, Carla, Joe, Dwight, or Todd. Nobody poisoned you or Kimberly or anyone else. You've been pointing fingers to cover up what happened at the Barn. I saw you. I saw both of you. You partied too hard, you took some drugs, and Kimberly passed out. Everything else, all of it, is a lie."

Kimberly took a step back and fell off the choir riser. Darci's lips grew thin.

"You're a liar. You're probably in on it," Darci spat.

"You had Joann's purse earlier, and you put the drugs in there yourself. They're going to have your fingerprints on them."

"You put your faith in science, but I'll put my faith in belief." Darci raised her hands, palms up, and one of the producers, who had more than a small sense of drama, made sure one of the lights was on her so it looked like a beam of sunlight.

Darci and I stood face-to-face.

"You want this to be about belief?" I turned to face everyone. "You don't need to believe me. You need to believe yourselves. Do you think Joann would do this? Do you?" No one said anything for a beat; Colin pushed through the crowd and stood next to Joann. He took her hand.

"I was at the Barn that night with Emma. We both

saw what happened. Everything she says is true."

"Oh, big deal," Darci said. "He's Joann's boyfriend, of course he's trying to defend her."

Justin, Darci's boyfriend, took a step forward. "And I'm *your* boyfriend. And I'll say they're telling the truth. I was there with you."

"Me too," said Richard.

Kimberly went to stand with them. She couldn't say anything. She was crying too hard.

"Darci?" Reverend Evers asked, his voice soft.

Darci looked between the crowd that stood in front of her and her dad. Her face was flushed, and her hair was starting to fall limp. People in the crowd were whispering to one another. The producer on the sidelines was flipping pages madly, trying to find some way to get back on track. Reverend Teaks took matters into his own hands, or to be more precise, he took me into his hands. He grabbed me by both shoulders.

"Praise God! He has seen fit to bring us the truth through the mouths of babes."

I yanked away from him.

"Your God . . . isn't mine."

I didn't wait for him to say anything else. I walked toward the door. I could hear the producer yelling for them to go to commercial. People in the crowd were calling out to one another, and Kimberly was still crying.

I didn't stop for anyone; I walked straight through, the crowd opening up before me until I was outside the tent in the fresh air.

35

God, I'm not sure what you would do if you were living my life, and I'm going to stop worrying about it. It's time to make my own decisions. From now on it's a case of WWED: What would Emma do?

"Hey, wait up."

I turned, and Colin was coming out of the tent after me. He shuffled to a stop when he got close.

"What you just did was a good thing," he said.

"Yeah, sometimes things have a way of working out."

"I'm sorry about everything."

"Me too."

"Joann wants to talk to you. She feels bad."

"She shouldn't. She's right, I haven't been a great friend. I treated my stuff as more important than hers. I owed her one."

"What about Todd?"

"What about him?"

"You guys going to go out now?"

"I don't know. I'm not sure he'll give me another chance."

"He'd be an idiot not to."

"Maybe I'll get you to tell him that," I said, giving Colin a smile. It felt right between us again, for the first time in a long time. "Maybe you could flash him that bathtub photo. I'm topless in that one."

"You know, school rules mean they're going kick you off the track team." Colin kicked at the dirt ruts, setting a puff of dust up into the air. We both watched it for a moment.

"I figured as much."

"Will Northwestern offer a full ride if you don't finish the season?"

"I don't know. I guess we'll see."

"I'm sorry."

I shrugged. A few hours ago I thought the chance at the track scholarship was everything. Now I wasn't so sure.

"What are you going to do?" Colin asked.

"Long term?"

He nodded. I looked out across the field. People were starting to leave the tent. Guess the show was over. The sun was just starting to set.

"I don't know what I'm going to do long term, but for right now?" I looked at him. "Right now I'm going to go for a run."

"A run?"

"You take care." I leaned over and gave Colin a kiss on the cheek, and then I turned away and started running.

The first few steps were hard, the way they always are, but I found my stride and started to pick up speed. I raised my arms straight out and felt the air rush by. For the first time I wasn't running from anything, I was running toward the future, without fear, only exhilaration. And I had no idea what would happen next.

Acknowledgments

"Acknowledgments" is just a fancy way of saying "Whoa, I totally couldn't have done this without you," and I have a whole bunch of people who fall into that category.

I have to thank my parents, who always encouraged me to read and clean my room. Turns out both were skills I needed. To the rest of my family, thanks for giving me so many fun things to write about.

I am lucky enough to have great friends. Big thanks to all of you for all the support, shared laughs, and offers of chocolate when needed. To Jamie, who always reads the first ugly drafts—I owe you one. Over the past year I've had a chance to meet some great writers who have offered me all kinds of advice and never once made fun of me (at least, not to my face). Thank you.

My agent, Rachel Vater, I owe for always cheering me on and being an amazing business partner. Working with the entire team at Simon Pulse has been fantastic. Special thanks go to my editor, Anica Rissi, who made this book so much better than I could have on my own. I would write for her anytime.

To everyone who picks up this book and gives it a read, I know there are many books to choose from so I appreciate your giving this one a chance. Drop me a line at eileen@eileencook.com and let me know what you think.

Lastly, I owe my two dogs for keeping me company while I write, and Bob for always believing this was possible.

About the Author

Eileen Cook spent most of her teen years wishing she were someone else or somewhere else, which is great training for a writer. When she was unable to find any job postings for world-famous author, she went to Michigan State University and became a counselor so she could at least afford her book-buying habit. But real people have real problems, so she returned to writing because she liked having the ability to control the ending. Which is much harder with humans.

You can read more about Eileen, her books, and the things that strike her as funny at www.eileencook.com. Eileen lives in Vancouver with her husband and two dogs and no longer wishes to be anyone or anywhere else.